MR. NOVEMBER

HEROES OF ROGUE VALLEY: CALENDAR GUYS
BOOK 11

ANN ROTH

MR. NOVEMBER—DANIEL O'DWYER

Age 30, 6'4" tall, 200 lbs.
Widower and Single
Firefighter.
Time with Guff's Lake Fire Department: 2 years

1

———————

Sarah McCone was excited when her ten-hour shift as a dispatcher for the Guffs Lake Fire Department ended Tuesday afternoon. Instead of heading for home, she drove three minutes up the road to the fire station to meet with Daniel O'Dwyer, aka Mr. November on this year's calendar. She barely knew the firefighter—he'd only been with the department two years—but the swoon-worthy male was very much on her radar. They'd officially met once, when he'd visited the dispatch center to meet the people who worked with their station.

One glance and she'd been hooked like a fish.

He wasn't the handsomest man in the hunky crew of firefighters, but to Sarah's mind he was the most attractive. Besides being big and muscled as most of the team was, he had gorgeous copper-brown hair, clipped short. The color somehow brought out his eyes, onyx, she called them, that hinted at sorrow and made her want to know more. The eyes, his proud, prominent nose, chin that jutted out a fraction, and wide mouth that rarely cracked a smile added real character to his face.

The very thought brought on a lovesick sigh. She'd

had a crush on him since he'd joined the department. He had no idea, of course, and neither did anyone else except Erin, the bestie who shared her little house, and two close friends at the dispatch center.

They were supposed to meet at five-fifteen to collaborate on the emergency preparedness class he'd scheduled for the following week, but due to a fire call that'd come in several hours earlier, he was likely to be running late.

As she'd expected, he texted a few minutes later. *Looks like I won't get back for at least another hour. Reschedule for tomorrow?*

Not only running late, but postponing. She was both disappointed and relieved. Disappointed because she'd so wanted to meet with him today. Relieved because she was exhausted and super hungry. She wolfed down a granola bar before replying. *I'm off Wednesdays, so that works. Where and when?*

Meet at Rosemary's for breakfast? My treat.

What time?

My shift ends at seven. How about seven-thirty? Too early?

He wasn't the only one with grueling hours. With four ten-hour shifts a week, and Wednesdays and weekends off, she'd planned to sleep in tomorrow. Still, considering her usual wake-up time was four o'clock in the morning, an extra hour or so would do. *Sounds good. See you there.*

She texted Erin to let her know she'd be home earlier tonight than expected. By the time she reached her car, her roomie had texted back that she was working late, as she often did at the Animal Care Clinic, and was meeting her boyfriend, Flick, for dinner, then a movie. In other words, a late night.

Not in the mood to be alone, Sarah stopped at The

Rogue, a restaurant similar to Denny's only with tastier food, and ate at a table for one. Better to be around strangers than go home and feel lonely, which she was, far too often.

~

In Daniel's opinion, Rosemary's Breakfast Nook served the best breakfasts in town. When the team's shift ended Wednesday morning, he and any crewmates interested in a tasty start to the day headed there to eat. The café was only a few short blocks from the firehouse, and getting there by car or on foot was easy. The Nook always welcomed them, and posted the calendar prominently above the display case. Today, Hank, Max, Rob, and Liam headed there on foot with him.

"I won't be sitting with you guys this morning," he told them on the walk over. At this hour, the air was frosty with a heavy cloud cover, normal for early November in the Rogue Valley. "I'm meeting with Sarah McCone over breakfast."

Rob, one of his closest buddies, nodded approvingly. "Ah, the upcoming Emergency Preparedness class. Why this morning?"

"We're both off today, and I want to meet before my appointment with a client at ten o'clock." When not doing his 48-hour shift at the firehouse, Daniel spent time detailing cars for the business Rob had started before Daniel had relocated from Sacramento and the curveball that—not wanting to go there, he shoved the painful thoughts of the past away.

"Interesting you're meeting with her about that when you already know so much," Rob said. "But smart."

"Exactly. She's full of great info and sees possible disasters from a different view than we do. I want that perspective."

"When I joined GLFD a few years before you, I did the same thing," Hank said. "She knows a lot."

As always, the Nook smelled of good food and strong coffee. Shortly after they stepped inside, Sarah entered. Having met her when he'd first joined the department and seen her at some of the goodwill functions the firehouse sponsored, Daniel recognized her and beckoned her over. She was bundled up in a parka and a bright-pink knitted cap.

"Morning," he said, his greeting echoing those of the other guys.

"Good morning." Sarah pulled off the cap. Due to static electricity, fine strands of her blonde hair floated around her crown. It was cute. "Brr, it's cold out there."

Rosemary, plump with a toothy smile, bustled toward them. "Table for six?"

Daniel shook his head. "Sarah and I have a breakfast meeting scheduled."

He swore she blushed. Nah, had to be the sudden warmth after the cold that put the color in her cheeks. The restaurant owner nodded and directed them to a table on the far side of the café. The other guys headed for a bigger table closer to the entry.

"I haven't been here in years," Sarah commented, as she hung her jacket on the back of her chair and sat down.

The second he joined her, he bumped her knees with his. He scooted his seat back some. "Sorry about that—I have long legs."

"So I noticed. This place smells so good, my mouth is watering." She studied the menu.

"Me, too—every time." In the awkward silence, he cleared his throat. "Did you walk from home?"

"How did you know?"

"Your cheeks are red."

"Are they?" She cupped her palms to her face. "I sit most of the day at work and try to get outside when I can. I'm not that far from here, only a few blocks east of Main Street." Which was about six blocks from the station and another few from Rosemary's.

"That's a good walk. Nice location."

"It's close to the dispatch center. How about you?"

"I live about a twenty-minute drive west."

A middle-aged waitress stopped at the table with a pad and pen at the ready. Sarah ordered an omelet, pancakes, and bacon, and Daniel wide-eyed her. "That's a lot of food."

There went her cheeks again, flushed pink. "I'm hungry. Don't worry, I won't waste one bite. I'll take any leftovers home."

"I'm not criticizing, I'm surprised. You're tiny."

"High metabolism. I'm lucky that way. You ordered a lot, too. That breakfast special is huge."

He shrugged. "I'm a big guy."

The coffee arrived. "Do you want to work while we eat?" she asked.

"Let's enjoy our food first. If it gets crowded, we'll have to order something else so we aren't forced to rush."

"I have errands to run and can't stay too long," she said.

"So do I." She had pretty eyes, hazel and gold, if he wasn't mistaken.

"Why are you studying me?" she asked with a slight frown.

Was he? Hadn't meant to put her on the spot. "I

don't think I've seen hazel eyes with gold ringing the pupils."

"As far as I know, it's common. The color changes depending on the lighting or what I'm wearing, so maybe it's extra noticeable? Yours are onyx, I think."

"Is that what they're called. To me, they're plain old dark brown."

"Okay, but I'm sticking with onyx." Her expression shifted and her lips curled into a smile that brightened her whole face. He felt the vague stirring of something long dormant—physical attraction. Immediately after he acknowledged the thought, guilt struck. Kendall had been gone almost three years, yet he couldn't look at a woman without his conscience pricking him. Penance for the past, a yoke his brain refused to relinquish, and the reason he'd tried dating only twice since moving to Guff's Lake.

"Suddenly, you look so serious," she said.

He didn't want to get into that, didn't talk about it. Lucky for him, the food arrived, and he was saved from replying. After a few bites, he felt okay again.

"You seem better now," she commented.

"I was running on empty." Which was true, but not the whole story.

"Me, too. This is delicious." She ate with gusto, the same as him.

The conversation was mostly chitchat about this and that. She was more relaxed now and easy to talk to—witty and animated. Not what he'd expected, but then, he hadn't really thought about it. He told her about his dog, Toad. She laughed when he explained that the animal's ability to hop like a toad when excited had led to the name.

She talked about her roommate, who worked for the same vet where he took his dog. Small world. After ordering more coffee, they set to work on the class. Hank had been right—she had great ideas. He added *smart* to the list of things he liked about her.

When they finally finished and he settled the bill after refusing her offer to pay her share, they gathered their stuff together and stood. His buddies had gone, and he hadn't even noticed. Huh.

He offered her a ride home. She declined, and a good thing—he just had time to pick up Toad from Jenny's. She was Rob's ex and boarded his dog and others during the team's forty-eight-hour shifts. He'd take the pooch with him to his appointment to detail a sweet BMW 3.

On the way to the location of the vehicle, he thought about Sarah. He'd enjoyed getting to know a little about her. The truth was, he wouldn't mind learning more. She wasn't wearing a ring. Was she dating anyone? Not his business. Quickly dismissing his curiosity, he set to work.

And ordered himself not to think about her again.

2

Walking home from Rosemary's and bursting to tell Erin about the breakfast meeting with Daniel, Sarah phoned her. "I know you're about to leave for work, but I really want to talk to you. If you have time."

"Of course, I do. It's not every day my roomie has a one-on-one with Daniel O'Dwyer. I'm so jealous. I've met him exactly twice, when he brought his dog in for shots. Everyone in the office, men included, sat up taller and envied the dog he paid so much attention to. Tell me everything. Did you find out why he sometimes looks sad?"

"The subject didn't come up, and I wasn't about to ask," Sarah said, as she checked for traffic before crossing the street. "How could I, when I barely know the man? He didn't seem that sad this morning except for moments here and there." During those times, he'd gone quiet and had worn a far-away expression as if reliving something that caused him pain. And yes, her curiosity had spiked. "The rest of the time, he seemed fine, and actually cracked a few smiles." In those moments, he'd become even more attractive than he already was.

"You brought that out in him," Erin commented, sounding pleased for her.

Sarah doubted she'd had anything to do with those cheery moments. "Maybe he lightens up when he's away from work or because he's free for the rest of the week. I don't really know."

"Don't you want to find out why he gets so solemn? Maybe someone broke his heart, or someone he cares about is sick. It could be anything."

The only thing Sarah knew was he didn't wear a wedding ring, which told her he wasn't married. Unless he was and chose not to wear a band. "Yes, I'd like to know, but whatever the reason, it's really none of my business."

"You could ask him. If he doesn't want to tell you, he won't."

As much as Sarah liked her roommate, there were times when she got on her nerves. "Hello, it was a business meeting. I don't want to seem pushy, either, okay? Not counting the next public get-together sponsored by the Fire Department, I have no idea if and when I'll see him again." She wished they'd made plans to get together. Not that she expected anything like that with a man as smart and attractive as Daniel. Besides, as one of the guys featured in the calendar, there were probably tons of women interested in him.

Her father hadn't been wrong all those years ago, when she was eleven, and she'd overheard him tell her mom he didn't think Sarah was pretty. Her mother had mumbled something about looks not being everything, especially when puberty was just around the corner. Ouch. Sarah had studied herself in the mirror and had to agree—she fell far short of being pretty.

Not long after she'd eavesdropped and had her self-esteem shattered, her parents had divorced. Her mom packed up and left town with her and her brother Elton. They'd settled in Guff's Lake, where they'd been ever since.

By the time high school came around, Sarah had changed, growing from a skinny, gangly girl into someone more attractive. Not that it made much difference. She still lacked confidence, and for the most part boys weren't interested in her. The few who were didn't attract her in the least. The ones who did rarely returned the sentiment. Her mother had never been an affectionate person, and working to support their little family and juggling the bills hadn't helped. The distance between them remained even now. Sarah wished they were closer, but it was what it was.

"I don't expect to hear from Daniel," she added, wishing the opposite were the case. "I could tell he didn't see me that way." Except once or twice, when he'd talked about his dog and when she'd teased him about the color of his eyes. Then he'd grinned and beamed genuine warmth. Mostly though, he'd been all business.

"You're still crushing on him, though, right? I don't blame you. He's hot."

Sarah sighed. "As we both know."

"His dog's cute, too. If I were you and single, I'd go after him. Making the first move hasn't hurt me any. Some guys need a little prodding. Flick sure did. I wouldn't be dating him if I hadn't asked him out."

Erin's current boyfriend was good-looking and seemed like a great guy. Sarah envied her, but she was no fool and wasn't about to become one. "That's not for me."

"Suit yourself, but at least think about it. I have to leave for work right now, or I'll be late."

"See you tonight?"

"No, I'll be at Flick's again. Don't worry, I'll come back home soon."

~

KNITTING WAS Sarah's favorite way to relax. Every year for a while now, she'd knitted hats, scarves, and sweaters as holiday gifts for friends and relatives. This year, she'd agreed to sponsor a needy family of four for Christmas. They'd each get hats and scarves, of course, but she wanted to do more, giving them a grocery gift card and toys for the kids. As a dispatcher, she made a decent living and even had a savings. But having grown up with a mother who constantly struggled to keep a roof over their heads, she wasn't about to use the savings except for emergencies. What she needed now was a cash infusion to make the family's holiday especially bright.

She knew just how to earn the money—rent a booth during the annual holiday craft fair at Guff's Lake Community Center and sell knitted items. The craft fair ran only on weekends from Thanksgiving through Christmas, with one exception being the Friday after Thanksgiving. All items were handmade, and business was usually brisk. She'd done it before and had made good money.

As soon as she got home, she started her trusty Civic and headed for Deb's Knitting Store. It was a bit of a drive to the south side of town, but Deb's was her go-to for yarn, patterns, and other knitting-related items. Sometime later, toting two large bags of yarn skeins and patterns, she left the store. It was a clear, coolish day, perfect weather to be outside. How could she be anything but happy? Humming and eager to get knitting, she started toward the car, which she'd parked a few blocks from Deb's to squeeze in another walk.

She was almost there when a pitiful meow stopped her in her tracks. By its soft cry, it sounded young and scared. Where was the sound coming from? She couldn't tell. Unable to see any animals, she set her purse and bags on the sidewalk and began to check the bushes. All the while, the cries continued. "Where are you?" she called out in a singsong voice in an attempt to avoid frightening it.

She was hunkered down and peering through the bushes when something fell from a nearby tree and almost hit her. Of all things, an acorn. By this time of year, there weren't many left to fall. Squinting, she glanced up. She spotted a kitten, perched on a branch a good fifteen feet above her. "There you are," she said and scrambled to her feet. How was she supposed to get the little thing down? If only Daniel or one of the other firefighters were here. They'd know what to do. She'd call the station right now. "I'm going to call for help, all right?"

She was reaching for her purse and the phone when someone came up behind her. "It's only been a few hours since we had our meeting." Right away, she recognized the slightly husky voice. Daniel, as if she'd somehow summoned him. "What are you doin' here?"

She pivoted toward him. "Same question. Is that Toad?"

"In the flesh. I picked him up from Jenny's right after our breakfast meeting, then headed to this part of town to detail a customer's car. The weather's great and I was about to go home and take him out running when I spotted you."

"I can't believe you're here." She was so relieved to see him, she did something totally uncharacteristic—threw her arms around him just long enough to feel the gorgeously solid chest under his shirt and jacket before she caught herself and backed away. "Sorry, I didn't mean to do that." Her face burned with embarrassment. She longed to rush to her Civic a block away and flee, but the kitty needed help.

Daniel seemed equally uncomfortable, shoving his hands into the pockets of his jacket despite the leash looped around one hand. *Daniel O'Dwyer, Carver's Mobil Auto Detailing* was printed on the jacket. He detailed cars, too?

The midsize canine gave a soft *woof* and wagged his tail—as if begging for attention. She patted him in greeting. "Hello there, Toad," she said. The animal licked her hand, and she laughed. "I like you, too. What breed is he?"

"Collie mix of some kind. I don't know what else, though."

"You're a pretty boy. I hear you hop sometimes."

"He sure does, but not when he's leashed up. What's going on?"

"I was about to call the fire station. There's a kitty stuck up there." She gestured toward the upper branches.

"So I see. I'd best bring it down."

"How? It's pretty high up, and I doubt you have a ladder with you."

"You'd be surprised what I can fit in the trunk of my RAV4. Hang tight—I'll put Toad in the car and be right back."

His car, a shiny black affair, was parked on the street, not far from hers. Moments later, he returned carrying a metal ladder and a pair of gloves. He proceeded to un-fold and set it against the tree. After donning the gloves, he clambered up, all grace and skill. She sighed with admiration and watched as he scaled the branch where the kitty was and slowly approached it. He made a clicking sound with his tongue. "Come here," he said, his voice low and calm. Amazingly, the animal obeyed, went straight into his arms. He brought it down.

As soon as he and the kitten reached the ground, Sarah released the breath she'd been holding. "Thank you."

"Happy to help. By the look of him—or her—hang on," he said and gently lifted its tail. "A female. My guess is, she's a stray. She's not afraid of people, at least not yet, but she's dirty and skinny."

"I wonder who owns her?"

"No idea. Where do you want to take her?"

Sarah hadn't thought that far ahead. "A kitty rescue place?"

"They don't usually take strays and will probably refer you to animal control or a shelter if there's room."

Animal control sounded ominous. "What do you recommend?"

"Depends on what you want."

"I don't have an answer for that, except that I don't want her to end up living on the street or be eu-thanized."

"Make 'found kitten' signs and put them up every-where. Or post a photo on social media."

"Good ideas, but meanwhile, she has to go some-where." Not wanting to further bother him when he likely had better things to do, she made a decision. "My roommate, Erin, might know."

"That's right, she works at the Animal Care Clinic."

"Would you mind holding the kitty for a minute? I want to put my bags in my car." She grabbed her bulging knitting sacks in one hand and pulled out her cell phone on the way.

hardly knew anything except she knitted for the craft fair and that she seemed to have a soft spot for cats in need of help. He nodded at the hot-pink cap on her head, which she'd worn to breakfast. "Did you make that?"

"I did." She smiled. "I love bright colors."

He'd never have guessed. The few times he'd seen her in person, she'd worn what he called 'business casual' stuff and a name badge. He couldn't recall if her clothes had been unusually bright. Now he was curious. Only because he enjoyed learning new things about people he liked, and he definitely liked Sarah McCone—as a possible friend. "Pink suits you. You wouldn't have any problems standing out in a crowd."

"You sound like my mother. She's not a fan. According to her, bright colors are an obvious call for attention." She made a face.

"What's wrong with that?"

"Exactly. You'd have to ask her."

"Well, I think it's fun."

She brightened considerably. "That makes at least two of us. Knitting relaxes me. With my stressful job, I need it. Would you mind loading the bags in my trunk?" She unlocked her car, which was bright blue and a short distance from his, and popped the latch. "Thanks," she said when he finished. "I have one more favor. Will you hold the kitten again while I call Erin? I need to make an appointment at the vet's to get the kitten checked out. Because I work every weekday except this one, I want to get it done today. Cross your fingers."

Seemed she was considering keeping the little feline, he thought as she stepped away. Too far for him to hear what was said while she was on the phone. Engaged as she was in conversation gave him time to

3

Judging by the way Sarah juggled the two crammed shopping bags plus her purse and a cell phone, she could use some help. Ready and willing, Daniel quickly caught up with her, kitten in hand. He'd help her out, then come back for his ladder and take Toad home. After two days at Jenny Carver's, Daniel had picked him up and brought him along and leashed him nearby while he detailed the Beemer. Now his sidekick was patiently waiting for his Wednesday run. Daniel had promised him and was looking forward to it.

Just as he caught up with Sarah, she lost control of the bags. They fell to the sidewalk and spilled out yarn. Lots of it in an array of colors, plus several other items. "Well, shoot!" she muttered, and bent down to collect the stuff.

"I'll take care of that if you hold the cat," he offered. "You sure have a lot of yarn." He'd never seen that much all at once.

"Deb's Knitting Store is the best place in town to stock up. Most of it is for knitted hats, scarves, and other things I plan to sell at the holiday craft fair."

"Cool. I didn't know that about you." As yet, he

openly study her. She had a variety of animated expressions—solemn, laughing, concern, and some he couldn't decipher. Emotions unchecked.

He thought about the all-too-brief moment she'd hugged him when he'd first run into her. Not counting his sister and mother back in Sacramento, he hadn't hugged a woman since Kendall. He'd enjoyed the brief press of Sarah's softness against his body all too much. Oddly, at the time he hadn't felt one moment of guilt, hadn't thought about his deceased wife at all. But now, he felt bad about that. What a head case he was.

Sarah glanced his way, and he knew she'd caught him staring. He turned his attention to the kitten nestled in the crook of his arm, her feline gaze pinned on his face. Some minutes later, she ended her phone call and returned to the car. "Erin talked to Dr. Gruen. He agreed to squeeze in an appointment for the kitty late this afternoon. We may be stuck there a while, as the clinic is pretty busy that time of day. I'm supposed to bring her in and fill in a questionnaire as best I can. When it's our turn, either Dr. Gruen or his assistant vet will run some tests and get her vaccinated. Meanwhile, I'm supposed to buy kitten food—they recommended a certain kind—and something to carry her in."

"You can find things like that in most any pet store. You'll need a kitty litter box, too."

"You've owned a cat before?"

He shook his head. "When my sister and her family got a tomcat, they bought a lot of cat paraphernalia." He hadn't seen them or his parents since he'd moved to Guff's Lake, and missed them. From time to time they talked on the phone, but the conversation was awkward, and for good reason. Within weeks after the funeral, they'd stopped mentioning Kendall, as if there'd been no wife, no accident. Instead, they'd dealt with the tragedy with silence and pitying looks. The subject had become the elephant in the room and still was. He'd moved to Guff's Lake to get away from all that.

Sarah was quiet a moment and looked thoughtful. "Maybe I'll just get a cardboard carrier and a can of food."

"Smart to try those things out before you spend more. Are you leaning toward keeping her?"

Instead of answering the question, she studied the kitten nestled so contentedly in the crook of his arm. "Look how adorable she is! There are bound to be people who want her. Or we'll find her owner, if she has one. I'll take photos of her and post them right away."

"What if no one comes forward?"

She flirted with a smile. "Then I guess I'll be stuck with a kitten."

With the sudden sparkle in her eyes, she didn't seem at all unhappy about that. Until their meeting over breakfast, he'd never noticed how pretty she was. He glanced away. "I knew it—you want her."

"I can't say for sure, but I'm leaning toward it. The cottage I rent allows pets, but I wouldn't take her in until Erin okayed it. One of the issues is that I work ten-hour shifts, four days a week. She usually works five eight-hour shifts, but there are times when she works later. I can't imagine us leaving this adorable girl alone for that long, even if she does sleep most of the time. She was a stray, and I want her to feel safe and loved."

The kitten had fallen asleep and was purring loudly. Dang, it was cute. "You don't have a way to secure her while you drive," he said. "I'll take you to a pet store in my car and drop you back here at yours."

Had he really offered to drive her? Yep, and for good reason: As a firefighter, even off-duty, helping others mattered.

"I can't ask you to do that. You've already done so much."

"Hey, I don't mind. Let me put the ladder away." After Sarah opened the passenger door and buckled in, he handed the kitten to her. Then he harnessed Toad in the back seat and started the RAV4. "The only thing left on my agenda is to take Toad out for a run later." He glanced in the rearview mirror. "Did you hear that, boy? I mean it."

Sarah raised her gaze from the kitten to look over her shoulder. "I swear, that dog is smiling. He's such a friendly fella. Yes you are, Toad," she crooned. "Now he's sniffing and wagging his tail. Maybe he smells the kitten. She's very tiny," she told the dog, lifting the baby for him to see. Toad let out a soft *woof*. As if on cue, the kitten meowed in return. Sarah laughed, and Daniel couldn't help but grin.

"You're already friends, aren't you?" she said, in a honeyed voice that washed over him like a warm hug.

"I can't drive until I know where to go," he said, and pulled out his phone. "Give me a minute to find the nearest pet store." As he punched in the request, got the address, and it appeared on the car screen, the kitten let out a demanding meow. "I think she's hungry. Better scoot."

"Oh, dear." Sarah looked worried. "I don't know how I'll ever repay you for this."

His body had a few ideas, all of them physical. A first since Kendall's death. He shoved any thoughts about that away. "Every time you dispatch an emergency at the firehouse, you help us do our jobs. That's repayment enough."

She was cooing at the purring kitten in her arms. The animal didn't know how good she had it.

Once in the car, Sarah commented, "Your seat is so far back. I never realized how long your legs are. You'd think after I bumped your knees under the table this morning, I'd have known."

"That's me, Mr. Tall."

The ride was fairly quick, a good thing with the hungry kitty on Sarah's lap. "We'll feed you soon, I promise," she said over the mewling. "She's a pretty color gray, don't you think?"

"She'll be even prettier when she's cleaned up. I like the white chin, too. Toad was a rescue pup, weren't you, boy? If you're going to get a pet, it's a great way to go."

"I'll take your word for it. I've never had a pet of any kind."

Having had a variety of them during his childhood, he couldn't believe his ears. "No way."

"My father wouldn't allow it. He's an Army man, and we moved a lot. It was hard on animals, or so he said. Then when he left us, we barely had enough money to take care of ourselves, let alone an animal."

"What happened to him?"

"He met someone else. I was twelve and my brother Elton was nine. A year later, we moved to Guff's Lake. Mom stayed single until five years ago. Then she met Mason and remarried. She's happy now." She glanced at him. "I'll bet that's more than you ever wanted to know."

He didn't mind hearing about Sarah's life. "It's interesting. Good for your mom and her new husband."

A second marriage was fine for other people. For

him? The pain of losing Kendall was a powerful incentive to avoid it. "My parents are still married," he said. "They're in Sacramento, along with my sister and her husband and kids."

"That's right, you moved from there and took a job at our Fire Department."

"I was a firefighter there, too, for five years."

"I think I heard that. I'll bet you miss your family. What brought you here?"

"My wife passed away, and I wanted to start fresh."

He half wished he hadn't told her. Kendall's death was no secret, but talking about it brought out reactions he couldn't tolerate.

"I'm so sorry, Daniel."

Her face and voice were laced with sympathy, the kind that made him feel suffocated. Now he was stuck in the car with Sarah and her pity. "Mind if I turn on the radio?" he asked, and without waiting for a reply, found a station. Anything with music. The button he punched turned out to be new-age jazz. Perfect.

He didn't say another word.

POOR MAN WAS STILL GRIEVING and still in love with his wife, Sarah realized as Daniel drove in silence toward the pet store. That had to be the reason for the tension oozing from him and his buttoning up. By now, he was probably tired of her company, too—at times she talked too much—and about to lose his mind. Wouldn't be the first time, and a good reminder that she wasn't enough to interest a man as special as Daniel.

She should never have agreed to let him drive her. The kitten didn't seem to do much besides sleep, and she could've managed by herself. What she wanted now was to buy what she needed and get out of his way as quickly as possible.

For now, in an attempt to give him a modicum of privacy, she glued her attention to the passenger window and the trees lining that side of the road. Better that than chattering away like an idiot, pretending not to notice the uncomfortable finish to what had been an enjoyable conversation. The view was normal for early November, with most trees bare after shedding their leaves. The hardy firs and evergreens never did, though. The kitten mewled loudly, miserable little thing, almost as if she sensed the discomfort permeating the car.

At last Daniel signaled, slowed, and pulled into the pet store parking lot. Eager to get away from him and shop, she opened her door the second he braked to a stop. "Keep an eye on the kitty. I'll be back as soon as I can." She quickly exited the car.

It was just after noon, nice and quiet, and she was one of a handful of customers. A friendly clerk helped her find the supplies she needed. Following Daniel's suggestions, she bought a cardboard carrier, a litter box, cat food, and food and water bowls. If she ended up adopting the kitten, she'd buy whatever else she needed then.

To her surprise, when she returned to the car with her purchases, Daniel wasn't in the car and neither were the kitten or Toad.

Where had they gone?

4

———

The kitten complained a lot while Sarah was in the pet store, almost as if she missed her. On top of that, she was hungry. With no idea how long she'd be, Daniel left a note, letting her know the RAV4 was unlocked and that he, Toad, and the kitty would be back shortly. Hoping to calm the little loudmouth and give his dog a chance to move around, he leashed Toad, settled his unhappy rescue in the crook of his arm like he had earlier, and headed up the street. He needed to think, and walking around always helped, even with two animal companions. The feline quieted a bit but wouldn't relax until she ate something. "Soon," he promised.

He appreciated Sarah's sensitivity to his need for silence. Yet he also figured he owed her more of an explanation. Not the whole story, just enough.

When he returned to the car some minutes later, she was setting a bag of whatever she'd bought on the floor in the backseat on the opposite side of Toad's car harness. "I wondered where you were, but then I found the note on the windshield," she said. "Why did you decide to take a walk?"

"The kitten was yowling like crazy, and Toad and I figured moving around might help."

"Did it?"

"Yes, but not for long." The little thing was fully awake now and making increasingly loud complaints. Toad seemed to sympathize, his own crying noises joining hers. "How'd it go in there?"

"Fine. I got what I needed, including a dish with the bowls for food and water attached. I know you and Toad want to get home, but would you mind if I fed the kitten now? I'm not supposed to give her much, just a small amount, and see how it goes down."

Daniel imagined the cat throwing up or worse but wasn't going to worry about that now. She really needed food. "You'd better give her something before she breaks my eardrums. She has quite a loud voice."

"So I noticed. I don't think I should feed her on my lap. Any ideas?"

"How about on the floor between your feet? I'll harness Toad right away but wait to drive till she finishes." By the time he took care of that, the kitten was chowing down. "She's definitely hungry," he noted.

"Thirsty, too, I'll bet. Too bad the pet store doesn't sell water."

"I happen to have an unopened bottle of spring water in the glove compartment. Help yourself."

"Okay, and thanks," Sarah said, already opening it.

"Any time. Mind if we talk while we wait for her to finish?"

"Go ahead."

He cleared his throat. "I owe you an apology. I shouldn't have shut you out like that."

"I totally understand." She laced her hands in her lap and stared at them. "You lost your wife, a painful subject, but there I was, on the verge of talking away, asking questions that are none of my business. It makes sense you got tired of my company."

He couldn't have been more surprised or confused. He frowned. "That's not it at all." He had her attention now, her eyebrows arching a fraction. "I don't usually talk about Kendall—that was my wife's name." Sarah didn't say anything, simply let him explain. "We'd only been married four months when the accident happened. She was the love of my life and—" not wanting to get into the details, which would only cause questions he didn't want to answer, he paused. "She was driving through an intersection, and a car that should've stopped ran a red light. It was a front-to-side collision. Both she and the woman in the wrong died instantly."

Sarah bit her lip. "That's awful."

He swallowed hard and nodded. Kendall had been on the way to the hospital to pick him up after a second-degree burn from a fire that had sent him there. The accident wasn't his fault—he knew that—but that didn't change the what-if that constantly tore at him. If he'd let one of his crewmates drive him home instead, she'd be alive today. "This is why I don't talk about it. People look at me the way you are now. I don't want your pity."

"What I'm feeling isn't pity, it's sympathy," she said in a soft voice. "Hearing what happened hurts my heart. I can't imagine what it did to you."

Only someone who'd experienced the agony of an avoidable, sudden death would. He couldn't hide a wince of the pain that was still with him. Sarah reached across the bucket seat and laid her palm on his forearm. Feeling the pressure of that touch, even through his jacket and flannel shirt, comforted him.

When she withdrew her hand moments later, he missed the warmth. Also for some reason, talking about the loss made him feel better. Go figure.

"Thanks for telling me," she said. "Well, look at that. Little miss kitty is all done."

So was he. It was time to drop her and the cat off and head for home. "Ready to go?"

She nodded and scooped the tiny thing onto her lap. "I don't think I want to put her in the cat carrier until I take her to the vet this afternoon."

He drove back the way he'd come. The kitten didn't throw up or have an accident, a good sign. Not counting his firefighter buddies, most people talked and talked to fill in a silence, which seemed to make them uncomfortable. Not Sarah. She turned the radio back on at a low volume and seemed content. As was he. This time, the long stretch of silence between them was clear of the tension he'd felt before they'd reached the pet store.

As he neared the Civic, he shut the radio off and addressed what she'd said earlier. "FYI, I don't think you talk too much, and I'm not at all tired of your company."

He had the feeling she didn't buy it and wanted to change her opinion. "FYI, I don't say things unless I mean them. I enjoyed spending time with you at breakfast and the rest of this morning, including the talking. Rescuing the kitty felt good, too. Firefighters don't usually have time to climb a tree."

"You guys are super busy."

"Copy that."

"The perfect name for this little cutie just popped into my head."

"Yeah?"

"Her snowy white chin reminds me of a cotton puff. I'm going to call her Puff."

"Suits her nicely." He smiled. Sarah seemed pleased and comfortable again. "So you're leaning toward keeping her."

"If no one claims her, I will. When I get home, I'll post something on social media." She paused. "In a way, I don't want to."

"Then don't. We didn't see any posters about a missing kitten where we found her. If I had to guess, I'd say her mother either died or abandoned her. "I have a hunch you'll be a good kitty mom. Will you tell me how the appointment at the vet goes?"

"If you really want to know."

"Hey, I rescued her and carried her around. I'm vested in her outcome."

Her grin made the world seem brighter. He vowed to make her do that again soon. It didn't mean anything, he told himself, only that he considered her a friend worth getting to know better.

EVEN AT ALMOST FIVE O'CLOCK, the vet's office was full of humans with their caged animals, and Sarah expected to wait awhile. As was Erin's habit, she fluffed her blunt-cut brown hair, then checked her in and handed her a clipboard with a questionnaire of several pages. "Can I peek at her?"

Sarah nodded and opened the carrier. Her roommate sighed. "Aww, she's so cute."

"Right? I'm thinking maybe we'll keep her."

"I—" The owner of a patient who'd finished an appointment with Dr. Gruen was at the reception counter to pay up, and whatever Erin had been about to say was cut off. "We'll talk about that later," she said.

When they'd first rented their house, they'd dabbled with the idea of having a pet, discussing the pros and cons, but neither had a solid opinion and they'd put the question aside. Sarah had no idea what her roomie might say. She'd find out soon enough. For a while, she busied herself filling out a form with several pages and lots of questions. Ugh. Not long after she finished the chore and delivered it to Erin, an older woman entered the waiting area and placed her cat carrier on the vacant chair next to Sarah. "This is Marigold. Keep an eye on her while I check in," she said, and Sarah nodded.

Marigold. Where had she heard the name? While the woman was at the front desk, Sarah thought about that and recalled what Erin had told her. Marigold belonged to Mrs. Murphy, a woman who brought the cat in at least once a month with concerns about this and that. Each time, the animal turned out to be healthy. Erin and most of the staff figured she was lonely, as her husband had passed away the previous year.

Mrs. Murphy soon rejoined her and moved the carrier to the floor. She was talkative and friendly. "I don't have an appointment, but I hope Dr. Gruen or Casey, the veterinarian intern, can squeeze me in. I need to have my cat checked. She hasn't eaten much today, and I'm concerned. What about yours?"

"She's a kitten—I don't know how old. This morning, we spotted her way up in a tree, and my friend rescued her. We think she's a stray. I'm here to get her checked out and vaccinated and find out if she's healthy or in need of medication."

"That can be a worry." The chatty woman's hair

was streaked with gray and pinned back into a bun. "I think it's wonderful your friend was able to rescue her. I don't want to take someone else's seat." She glanced around. "Are they here?"

Sarah shook her head. "He's a firefighter and has other things to do, but this morning he happened to be free."

Her seat companion's eyes lit up. "I like firefighters. What's his name?"

"Daniel O'Dwyer."

"The man on the calendar," she nodded, looking impressed. "I've collected his and all the other autographs of those heroes. He's so attractive. Those dark eyes...I could swoon."

Imagine that, a woman old enough to be his grandma, having a crush on him. Sarah stifled a smile. Wait'll he heard about that. "He's a really good guy." Who was clearly pining for the love of his life. "Anyway, I've kind of fallen in love with this kitty."

"I know that feeling. I adore Marigold. She's part Siamese and talks a lot."

Just like her owner. "You must be Mrs. Murphy."

"That's right. How did you guess?"

"My roommate is Erin, the woman you just spoke to at the reception counter. She talks about some of the animals, and might have mentioned Marigold." Erin would die maybe of the giggles when she found out about the woman's crush. Of course, it paled in comparison with Sarah's.

She understood, though, that Daniel wasn't interested in her as anything other than an acquaintance. That was okay. She was no stranger of unrequited love. Sooner or later, most every man she'd been involved with moved on. It was a good thing she didn't love him. She simply liked him—a lot.

"Small world. I hope she didn't say anything bad about me."

"Not at all. She mostly talked about Marigold and what a sweetie she is."

"Sarah, Dr. Gruen is ready for you," Erin announced.

Sarah stood, and Mrs. Murphy waved her fingers at her. "I hope your kitty's okay."

"Thanks. Marigold, too."

She'd never met Dr. Gruen. He looked to be in his forties and had kind eyes. He was gentle with Puff and explained what he was doing as he went. After a thorough physical that included collecting blood samples for the tests he wanted to run, he proclaimed Puff a semi-healthy eight-week-old kitten.

"The test results should be back tomorrow," he said. "Then we'll get her vaccinated. She'll also need to be spayed. Standard protocol is to wait two weeks after the shots. You can schedule that while you're here. Erin will give you the details. Right now, she needs three to four meals a day to meet her nutritional needs, either dry or wet food. Make sure she eats. If she doesn't and seems listless or inactive, come back right away." He recommended a food brand he favored for kittens, which the clinic happened to sell, and suggested a follow-up appointment in a week or so to make sure she was gaining weight and discuss other things she'd need later.

Sarah bought enough food to last several days, then stopped by the reception counter to pay for everything and share the good news with Erin. "Of course, we have to wait for the results of the blood tests," she added.

"You never know how that will turn out," her friend said, "but I'm crossing my fingers." Another customer headed toward them, and Erin added in a low voice, "Change of plans tonight—I'm staying at Flick's again. I'll see you when I get off work tomorrow. We'll talk then."

Then no conversation tonight about whether or not her roomie was okay with keeping Puff. Regardless of the final decision, Sarah worked tomorrow and Friday. She needed someone to come over to check on and feed Puff while she was doing her dispatch thing. A bulletin board on the wall was full of information about obedience schools, pet sitters, and other stuff, and Sarah snapped photos of the names and numbers of people who might be able to help right away. Otherwise...she wasn't sure what she'd do.

On her way out, she stopped by where Mrs. Murphy was still sitting. Sarah's former chair was now occupied by a college-age male all but rolling his eyes as the gregarious older woman chattered away. "Everything looks good," she announced. "Now, I have to find someone to look in on her while I'm at work."

"What would that entail?"

"She's so little, she needs to be fed three or four times a day. I'll take care of that before and after work, but whoever agrees to do this will need to check on her and feed her in the afternoon at least once a day. Of course, I'll compensate them well." Sarah pulled out a piece of paper and jotted down her name and phone number. "If you know of anyone who might be available, please give me a call. And if you don't mind, share your number with me, too?"

Mrs. Murphy looked thrilled. "Happy to."

"Thanks, and I hope any news about Marigold will be positive." Kitty carrier in hand, she exited the clinic and wondered if she'd be able to line up someone to help. Fingers crossed.

An hour and multiple phone calls later, she had yet to find anyone on such short notice. In desperation, she decided to asked her mom, aka Lee, who didn't care much for animals. But Puff was so adorable...Pasting a smile on her face, she FaceTimed the woman and showed her the kitten while they spoke.

"Hi, Sarah," her mother said, and seemed pleased to hear from her. "We haven't talked for a while now. How are you?"

"Not bad."

"Is that a kitten you're holding?"

Sarah nodded. "Meet Puff. Isn't she the cutest?"

"She is. Is she yours?"

"Yes." Sarah hoped. She'd have to wait until tomorrow to find out if Erin was on board. "How's work?"

"Really good. As of this afternoon, I'll be working five days a week at the spa." Lee beamed.

She'd been a part-time receptionist at the spa in Guff's Lake Resort for several years now and wanted to work full time. "Good for you, Mom."

"Mason and I will be able to save up for a dream vacation—a Caribbean cruise."

Since marrying Mason some five years earlier, she'd mellowed considerably. "I'm not sure when the spa is open."

"Tuesday through Saturday, which gives me Sunday and Monday off. Why?"

"Puff is so little and underweight. The vet recommends feeding her three to four times a day, and I need a person to look in on her and feed her once or twice midday while I'm at work. Guess you won't be available."

"Sorry. Good luck finding someone."

Any second, the call would end. "Don't hang up just yet. Do you happen to know of anyone who might be interested? I'll pay them well."

Lee didn't, and Sarah blew out a sigh. Now what? She was beginning to panic. Daniel had asked for an update about the trip to the vet's. Maybe he'd know of someone who might be able to help.

5

Early that same evening, Daniel met Hank, Liam, and Tony at Marv's, a blue-collar diner and one of their favorite places for great burgers, beer, and pie. The place was always busy and noisy, in part due to the country-western tunes belting out from the old-fashioned juke box. While they waited for their pitcher and food, his cell phone rang. Sarah. He suspected she was calling to let him know what the vet had said and considered letting it go to voicemail and phoning her back later, but changed his mind. He'd been wondering since they'd parted ways hours earlier.

"I need to take this call where it's quieter and I can hear," he told his buds before he picked up. "Fill you in later." He stood up and moved out of earshot. "Hey," he greeted her.

"Wherever you are, it sure is noisy."

"Tell me about it. I'm having dinner with a couple of crewmates, but am on my way outside."

"I didn't mean to interrupt—"

"No big." He strode through the door and away from the noise. It was cold outside, and he'd left his coat on the back of his chair. Good thing he wouldn't be out here long. "Now I can hear you. How'd it go with Puff?"

"Thanks again for rescuing her and driving me to the pet store. Your coming along at just the right time feels like Kismet. I've been smiling about that all afternoon."

Although she couldn't see him, he grinned in return. "That's one lucky kitten."

"Uh-huh, and she's purring a lot about that. Anyway, as we suspected, she's likely a stray. I have good news and some not-so-good. I'll give you the positive first. She's about eight weeks old and seems more or less healthy so far. The results of the blood tests will tell us for sure. According to Dr. Gruen, we should have those tomorrow. If she's in good health, she'll get spayed."

"That won't be fun, but it's for the best. Thanks for the update." As eager as he was to return to the warmth of the diner, he wanted to hear the rest first. "And the not-so-good news?"

"I'm in a real bind and hoping you can help."

Having no idea what she was about to ask for, he braced himself. "Oh?"

"She's malnourished and should be fed three to four times a day, small amounts each time, until she's a bit older. An easy job if I didn't have to work, but with ten-hour shifts tomorrow and Friday, I won't be around to wake her to eat except in the morning and evening. In between, I need someone to come in and feed her. I've called a bunch of cat sitters, but at such late notice no one is available."

"What about a kitty daycare?"

"They won't take a cat without a clean bill of health, and with the test results unavailable until tomorrow at who knows what time, I'm in a bind. Even if

I had them, none of the businesses I contacted have openings on such short notice. Do you by chance know of anyone who might be available? I'll pay whatever the cost."

Daniel had no idea. Maybe Jenny Carver, although dogs were her thing. Sarah knew she boarded Toad and others when the firefighters pulled their long shifts. Still, she might know of someone who can look in on Puff. "I don't, but I'll run it by the guys I'm hanging with and get back to you. Maybe you should reach out to Jenny, too. I'll text you her contact info. Let's hope one of them will come up with a name. Can't your roommate help out?"

"She's at her boyfriend's tonight and I won't see her until she gets home from work tomorrow. We haven't had much chance to talk. I don't even know if she's okay with us having a cat in the house, but I do know for sure that she'll be at work tomorrow and the next day from nine till six and maybe later. I'll text her tonight and fill her in and ask if she can think of someone willing to help."

Looked as if for now, taking in the kitty permanently was up in the air. What would happen if the roommate nixed the idea? "Is there a friend you can ask to help you out?"

"Besides Erin, most of my friends work the same shift as me. I'll call Jenny right away. If I can't find anyone, I don't know what I'll do. I'd hate to take vacation days I haven't scheduled. The dispatch team needs me."

He knew how that felt. Barring unexpected personal illness or emergencies, firefighters rarely missed work they hadn't scheduled in advance. "I'll get back to you shortly." He returned to the diner. The pitcher had arrived, and one of the guys had filled his glass. He took a big sip but barely tasted the stuff.

"What's with the funny look on your face?" Liam asked. "Bad news?"

Daniel made a maybe, maybe-not gesture with his hand. "That was Sarah." While they'd waited for drinks earlier, he'd told them about the kitten rescue and what'd happened then, minus the hug and all that. It hadn't meant much—or so he'd reassured himself throughout the day whenever he thought about her—and he didn't want them getting ideas. "Test results depending, the kitten checks out okay, but she's malnourished and is supposed to be fed three or four times a day. We all know Sarah's work hours. She needs someone to stop by and feed the little thing but hasn't been able to find anyone. Any ideas?"

Hank stroked his chin, then shook his head. "None."

Liam and Tony also came up empty.

"Jenny might have ideas," Hank suggested.

"I mentioned that. Sarah's probably contacting her now. I'll let her know we're in the dark." Daniel stood again.

"Why not contact her after dinner?"

"That won't work. She's in a bind and needs someone tomorrow. I won't be long." This time he shrugged into his jacket as he headed outside.

"That's quick," she said when she picked up. "Do you have a name or two?"

"The guys came up blank. Did you talk to Jenny?"

"Yes. She doesn't know of anyone, either. I even asked my mom, but she just started working full time at the spa in the resort, which rules her out. I'm sure you'll meet her when you teach that class next week."

Sarah's heavy sigh was audible. "Guess I'll have to miss work."

He thought fast. Over the next two days, he had three car detailing jobs lined up. Otherwise, he was free. Tending a tiny kitten once or twice each day wasn't on his list of things to do in his spare time, but somebody had to lend a hand. "I can do that, but only this week. That should give you time to find someone else."

"Believe me, I'll try. You've already done so much for me and Puff. I can't impose on you anymore."

"No worries. I want that kitten to thrive."

"Aww, you like her as much as I do. Can you stop by later? I'll give you a spare key and show you how much to feed her. You won't have to spend time with her, just get her fed, give her fresh water if she needs it, and leave. I'll pay whatever you ask."

"I don't want your money, but I do want to eat dinner with my buddies now. It'll be a few hours before I stop by. Text me your address."

"I will. You're a lifesaver."

"So people tell me." He disconnected.

Not long after he rejoined his friends, the food arrived. "I'm extra hungry," Hank said. He started to dig in, then eyeballed Daniel. "Now, what's wrong?"

"My belly's as empty as yours. Let's talk and eat." After some minutes of silence to take the edge off, Daniel told the guys what'd happened. "I got roped into looking in on the kitten once or twice tomorrow and Friday."

"That explains the frown," Liam said. "You didn't have to say yes."

"Hard to say no when a friend's in a bind."

"I didn't realize you and Sarah were friends."

"After the time we spent together earlier? We definitely are. She has a roommate, but Erin works at the vet's and won't be home during the day. That leaves me."

"Don't tell me you have a thing now for kittens. Toad won't be happy."

Daniel thought about the furry little feline with the big blue eyes. "Trust me, I don't want a cat. My dog is all I need."

His companions exchanged looks. "What now?" he asked.

"You're interested in Sarah."

"Not that way." That he cared to admit, even to himself. "Did you not hear me say we're friends?"

Hank grinned. "That's how Deanna and I started." He'd met his girlfriend when a fire had all but destroyed the B&B she'd been restoring. He'd been on the team that had finally put it out, but not in time to save much of the building. "As far as we know, she's single. So are you."

By all appearances, but his conscience bothered him too much to start anything. He clenched his jaw and ignored the comment.

"Relax, man," Hank said. "I didn't mean anything by that, just pointing out the truth."

"Who wants pie?" Daniel said, and signaled the waitress. Within minutes, she delivered it.

"Then don't talk about why the idea of dating bothers you," Hank said, while they enjoyed the dessert.

Couldn't the guy lay off? Daniel snorted. "Look, I'm not ready to get involved, okay?"

"Yeah, you dated a couple of women a while ago and nothing worked out, but there are a whole lot more around here. At some point you gotta give it another try."

Lately, his irritating mother had begun to bring that up every time they talked—without a word about Kendall. "I'm aware of that." Liam opened his mouth to speak, but Daniel cut him off. "This conversation is over, and I need to get going. See ya."

LATER THAT EVENING, Sarah was playing with Puff, who'd gotten much more active after two small meals in her belly, when the doorbell chimed. Daniel had arrived at her house! She could hardly believe it. Way too eager to see him when she knew perfectly well he wasn't interested in her like that, she pushed her hair behind her ears, scooped up the kitten, and answered the door.

Although early November days tended to be on the cool side, tonight the cold fresh air that whistled in with him felt like winter. "Come in," she said, and gestured him through the door.

There wasn't much to the small house, and she observed him as he took in the living room and the hallways to the left and right. "Cute place."

"Erin and I really like it. We moved in about two years ago." The paint had been fresh, the carpets new, and the rent reasonable. Between them, they'd had just enough furniture to furnish the two bedrooms and add a table and chairs in the kitchen. They'd shopped second-hand stores for the pretty smoky-blue sofa and magenta chairs in the living room, and had found drapes that worked well with the colors. Throw in knickknacks and pictures on the wall, and the place truly felt like home. For now, at least. For all Sarah knew, Erin could easily decide to move in with Flick. Time would tell.

"If you don't mind playing with Puff, I'll hang up your jacket," she offered.

As if the kitten understood, she let out a meow and stared at Daniel with eyes that pleaded for him to hold her.

"Hey, Puff," he said in a gentle voice, as he slipped his jacket off and swapped it for the feline. She immediately crawled up his shirt, perched on his shoulder, and batted his chin.

He surprised Sarah with a chuckle, a charming sound she hadn't heard before. She couldn't help but smile and then sigh. The man was irresistible.

"You're a lot livelier than you were earlier today," he told the kitty.

"Food, water, and being in a warm, safe place help." Sarah liked that he didn't seem to mind having the tiny thing on his very broad shoulder. "I think she's glad to see you."

"The feeling's mutual. When Puff and Toad met, they seemed fairly comfortable around each other. Would it be okay to bring him with me when I feed her? Depending on the test results, of course. Hopefully, you'll get them early in the day."

"He's welcome here."

A full grin, broader than what she'd seen so far, bloomed on his face. He looked even handsomer than he was without it. Her foolish heart hammered in her chest, a waste of pounding. The smile was totally due to Puff and had nothing to do with her. Knowing so didn't affect her feelings in the least, except that she liked him more than ever. "I know you're busy and I don't want to keep you," she said, when what she really wanted was for him to stay awhile. "Let's say Puff tests out as healthy. What if she freaks out around Toad and he's not happy being together, either?"

"Then I'll take him back to the car to wait while I feed and water her."

"That works for me. I'll show you where things are and how much to give her.

Daniel nodded and looked at her. "You've been wearing your hair down today."

"I usually do when I'm not at work." Acutely self-conscious, she tucked it behind her ears. Where it only stayed if she used hairclips, something she hadn't thought about while she waited for him. "Is that bad?"

"No, I like it."

By the soft light in his eyes, he seemed interested in her. Sarah knew better. What she thought she saw was the result of her overactive imagination and strong desire for him to feel for her the way she did him. It was clear that his deceased wife owned his heart. She couldn't possibly compete with that. "Follow me to the kitchen, and I'll show you where things are," she said, and started forward.

He plucked Puff off his shoulder and cradled her tiny body in his big hand. Loud purring filled the air. "She really likes you," Sarah said, giving him a warm smile.

"I like her too," he said, looking at Sarah as if he meant *her*. Then he frowned, reached out with his free hand, and tucked the lock of hair that had freed itself behind her ear. "That's been bothering me. Now you can see out of both eyes."

"My hair has a will of its own, which is why I wear it pulled back at work," she murmured, unable to move or look away from his gaze. His hand grazing her face was mesmerizing, his fingers warm and gentle. He smelled good, too, a clean scent of some kind, as if he'd recently showered. During the two years of her crush, she'd had a number of fantasies featuring him, but nothing nearly as potent as a simple touch. There went her heart, thudding in her ears almost as loudly as Puff's purrs.

He cleared his throat, dropped his hand, and stepped back. Wishful thinking, that's all it was. Pretending she wasn't gaga over him, she showed him where she stored the food and how much to feed Puff.

With a reluctant glance at the kitten, he set her down. "This has been fun, but I have to go."

Sarah gave him the key. "Thanks so much, Daniel. I'll text you as soon as the test results are in. Whether Toad comes with you or not, feel free to let me know how it goes. And when you finish Friday, leave the key here in the kitchen."

"Will do. 'Night."

"Good night." Standing in front of the living room window with Puff in her hand, she watched his long legs stride toward the RAV4. Moments later, he was gone. An empty feeling followed, which she ignored. Puff, too, seemed sad that he'd left. "You'll get over it," she told the feline. "I'm going to text Erin right now about you, but I doubt I'll hear back." Listen to her, talking to a kitten is if it could understand.

After she sent the text, she got ready for bed. No word from Erin, and she figured they'd catch up the following evening.

"It's bedtime, and I have to get up early in the morning," she told Puff. The kitten gazed at her with an irresistible, earnest expression. "All right, you can share the bed, but please behave."

Of course, she woke Sarah continually, leaving her exhausted when the alarm jarred her awake.

"I'm buying you a kat playpen this afternoon," she announced in the morning. "From now on, that's where you spend your nights."

6

Midmorning Thursday, Daniel received a text from Sarah. Puff had tested negative for diseases, which was great news and cleared the way for him to bring Toad with him to her place. "Behave," he told his leashed dog on the way to the front door. Inside, tail wagging, Toad cautiously approached Puff. The kitten's back went up, but with the mutt keeping a respectful distance, she soon relaxed. She seemed happy to see Daniel, which charmed him, and he stayed to play with her for a little while. Toad observed with interest.

While there, he took note of details that had escaped him the previous evening. In contrast to his colorless apartment, her place had a cozy, friendly vibe. A real treat.

Friday was a repeat of Thursday, with the addition of several new purchases in the living room—a cat playpen with a blanket, likely for the kitten to sleep in, toys, and a scratching post. Apparently, she'd gone shopping the previous day after work. Her roommate must've agreed to keep the kitten.

He was pleased about that and happier still when Puff and Toad actually touched noses. He also liked how the kitten came running when the two of them entered the house. Sleep a lot or not, she was lonely, he guessed and didn't blame her. Being by yourself all day was hard for anyone, especially a very young kitten. He was used to the solo life, or had thought so before he'd gotten to know Sarah better.

Not that he knew that much. Yet, want to or not, he couldn't stop thinking about her. The softness of her cheek when he'd tucked her hair behind her ear, the whiff of sweetness he'd noted when standing closer. The way she'd sucked in a breath, as if waiting for something more.

He knew better than to think about that, yet the traitorous thoughts continued despite his pricking conscience. Best to leave now and get on with the day. But he got a kick out of Toad wagging his tail and Puff trying unsuccessfully to grab hold of it, and lingered. His phone rang, signaling a call from his mom. He sat down on the sofa and answered. "Hey, Mom."

"You busy?"

"Not right now. What's up?"

At that moment, Puff meowed.

"Did I hear a cat?" she asked.

"She's a kitten. Toad and I stopped by to feed her."

"Stopped by where?"

"A friend's." No telling what she'd say if she found out he was at a female's place.

"One of your teammates?"

"No, she's a—"

"She?" she said in a pleased, lilting voice. "About time you met someone."

Here we go. Daniel was irritated, but feigned nonchalance. "She's the dispatcher for the firehouse. We're friends, that's all."

"And you haven't told your dad and me, or Izzy and Cyrus?" His older sister and brother-in-law.

She didn't seem to have heard what he said, his irritation increased. "Don't start, Mom. I have things to do. I need to feed this kitten and leave."

"All right. But before you hang up, I wanted you to know that the whole family including your nephews are driving up for Thanksgiving."

Talk about caught off-guard. The idea of them coming to Guff's Lake put him on edge. Not that he didn't love them, but it'd been three years since Kendall's death, and they still tiptoed around as if it'd never happened. It was weird and uncomfortable, but not something he wanted to talk about over the phone or in an e-mail or text. Her blatant comments that he should get out there and meet a woman to settle down with especially irked him. "That's only a few weeks from now. What made you decide to come up here?"

"You don't come to us, so we'll come to you."

"I'm real busy here—you know that. If you're coming, flying might be faster. Sacramento is a good five-hour drive from Guff's Lake."

"We know that. Since your father and I last talked to you, Izzy and Cyrus bought a snazzy van. There's plenty of room to fit all six of us. It'll be fun."

Daniel wasn't sure about that. "Good for Izzy and Cyrus. Unlike their van, my apartment is tiny. Holidays in Guff's Lake tend to draw crowds from all over. I don't know that you'll find a place to bunk."

"You don't want us to come." His mother sounded hurt.

"It's fine, Mom, but where will you stay?"

"That's all taken care of. We booked rooms at the Willard Motel."

He'd never heard of the place. "I don't know anything about a Willard Motel. It could be a dump. If you'd let me know in advance, I'd have given you the names of several possible places to contact."

"This phone call is my notice that we're coming, Daniel. The Willard is reasonably priced and has decent reviews. And it's not far from the Guff's Lake Resort, which looks like a beautiful place. Your nephews are really excited, and so are the rest of us. We hope you'll find time to show us around."

His mom's unexpected announcement had sunk in, and he was beginning to look forward to the visit. "When my shift ends the Tuesday before Thanksgiving, I'll have plenty of time. "It'll be great to see you all. What about Thanksgiving dinner?"

"We can have it at your house, but if the kitchen's too small, we'll go out. Maybe you can get us a reservation someplace."

That could be a real headache. He had a hunch most restaurants in town were booked up but had no idea. "I'll get back to you on that—give me a day or two. I need to go—I have an appointment soon."

"To detail a car? Such a lucrative way to keep busy on your days off."

The call ended. Rather than contact Sarah by text or phone, he left a scribbled note similar to the one he'd penned the previous afternoon, reassuring her that Puff seemed great and that she and Toad seemed comfortable enough around each other. He couldn't help adding an additional line. *Just found out my parents, sister, brother-in-law, and nephews are driving up for Thanksgiving.* He couldn't have said why he needed to mention that.

Before taking off, he left her key on top of the note and mentally brushed his hands together. He'd helped Sarah out; now to tackle that car that needed detailing. Then drop Toad at home and grab something to eat, and head for the standing Friday night poker game. Hanging with guys he worked with at the station, smoking cigars, guzzling beer, munching on junk food—what could be better? He never knew how many would show up, but he always had a good time that was guaranteed to keep his mind off both Thanksgiving and Sarah.

POKER THAT NIGHT was at Ethan's place. Daniel showed up psyched and ready to have fun, but besides him, only Nate showed. "Tiny group tonight," the dude commented. "The pot will be smaller than usual, but it'll still be fun. Let's each put in five dollars this week. I'm in the mood for Texas Hold-'em. You?"

Fine with both Daniel and Nate. They anted up, lit cigars, popped open cans of beer, and dug into the snacks. With fewer guys, the games didn't take long. They stretched the evening out cracking jokes and sharing stories about their off-duty jobs and whatever else came up. Things were good till they started talking women. "Kiley and I are thinking about moving in together," Ethan said. His girlfriend had started Cluster Busters, a thriving business that helped people organize their homes—including Ethan's.

Nate's brows went up. "That happened fast."

Way too fast, Daniel thought but kept that to himself.

Ethan grinned. "When you know, you know. I predict you and Becca will be next." Nate and his girlfriend had been a couple for several months now.

"It's too soon for us. Maybe in the future."

Attention turned to Daniel, and Ethan commented. "Are you ever gonna tell us about rescuing a stray cat a few days ago, or that Sarah McCone was with you?"

The rescue was no secret, but Daniel hadn't mentioned it. "I figured I didn't need to, and that Hank, Liam, or Tony would fill you in."

"They did. How did you come to rescue a cat, and where does Sarah fit in?"

He repeated what he'd told the other guys. "You should see that little fluff ball," he finished. "She's about eight weeks old and tiny enough to fit in my palm. Sarah named her Puff for her white chin."

"So you're into cats now, and a woman. It's about time, and I'm not talking about felines."

Daniel scoffed. "I don't need another mother pushing me to meet somebody. Anyway, it's not like that." But he'd sure thought about it. So much for keeping his mind off Sarah tonight. "I didn't plan to run into her. We happened to be in the same part of town, and I saw her staring up at something in an oak. She was worried about the kitten trapped up there and needed help getting her down. I was there and offered to do the job. End of story." At least as far as he intended to say.

But his buds weren't finished. Ethan squinted at him. "You said I sound like your mom. What does she have to do with any of this?"

"She phoned earlier to invite herself and the rest of the family up for Thanksgiving and hinted that it was time I meet someone."

"Talk about pressuring a guy." Nate puffed on the last of his cigar. "How many are coming?"

"My parents, my sister and husband, and my two nephews."

"Six people plus you. Sounds like a doable crowd. How old are the boys?"

Daniel thought a moment. "Six and eight."

"You never mention your family. Cool that they're coming to visit. Will this be their first time in Guff's Lake?" Daniel nodded, and the dude eyeballed him. "What's with the frown?"

"They dropped this visit on me with no advance warning, that's what. Now I have to find a place for Thanksgiving dinner. Do either of you know of anything?"

Both guys shook their heads and suggested he get busy on the phone.

"What am I gonna do with them before and after that?"

Ethan gaped at him as if he'd lost his marbles. "You've lived here two years and have to ask? Do the tourist thing and show them around—duh. You haven't seen your nephews in a while, and I'm sure they'll like visiting the station and wherever else you take them. This is a chance to get to know them and catch up with the rest of the family." He paused. "The whole thing sounds fun to me."

"You don't go down to Sacramento, either," Nate chimed in. "They're your family, man. What've you got against them? Not that it's any of my business."

"For starters, they're as nosy as you two." Not wanting to get any further into it or bring up Kendall, Daniel shut his mouth.

"Relatives can be exasperating for sure," Ethan said, and returned to the cat rescue. "In my thirteen years with the department, I've had exactly one opportunity to rescue a cat. It was kind of fun."

"Same here," Ethan said. "The only time I did it,

people gathered around, watching and cheering when I brought the animal down."

"A first for me, too," Daniel said. "It's an experience."

"No collar on the cat or ID?"

He shook his head. "She's about eight weeks old. I don't know how she navigated her way up that tree, but she did. We think she was a stray. Skinny, dirty, hungry, all that. No missing cat notices anywhere in the area. Sarah took her to the vet's for a checkup. As far as I know, she's gonna be okay."

"She's planning on keeping it, huh?"

"That's right, and I don't blame her. She named it Puff, and she's awful cute. She said something about talking to her roommate about keeping it first. I assume that went well. The kitten's supposed to eat three to four times a day to gain strength and energy. Sarah works long hours and couldn't find anyone to feed her during the day. She was in a real bind, had to work Thursday and today, so I stopped by her place and did the feeding. Puff's doing all right. She and Toad have got along."

Both men looked surprised. "You did that?"

"Yep. Sarah spent her Wednesday morning helping me with the class I'm teaching next Tuesday, and this was a way to pay her back. It was only the two days and took under thirty minutes. From now on, someone else will do it."

"You like her," Nate observed.

How had he guessed? "What makes you say that?"

"Your face changes when you talk about her."

Was that true? Daniel didn't like that, and didn't want anyone getting the wrong idea. He gave a casual nod. "I do like her. She's good people."

"I don't know her well, but from the way she works

the dispatch and the friendly smiles she has when she shows up at the events we sponsor, that tracks. Gonna ask her out?"

Some people...Daniel scowled. "I don't think so, not that it's any of your business."

Ignoring the 'butt-out' look, Nate pressed on. "If you like her, why not?"

"Give it up, will ya? I'm not ready."

"You don't have to get all testy about it," his buddy grumbled.

"Yeah, lighten up," Ethan chimed in. "We're interested because you're family, like we all are at the firehouse. We care, okay?"

Pulling weekly forty-eight-hour shifts together linked them like brothers. "And I get that," Daniel said. "Doesn't mean I want to talk about it."

"But you do understand we're aware you've been alone since you moved here, and—" Ethan cut himself off. "Never mind. Your private life is none of my business unless you want it to be."

"I don't." Daniel checked his watch. "Time for me to split. Congrats on winning the pot tonight, Nate. See you jokers Monday."

When he got home, he let Toad into the fenced yard to do his thing. Then, needing a friendly ear about his family's plans to come to Guff's Lake, he phoned Sarah.

7

Friday evening, Sarah got an unexpected call from Mrs. Murphy. Maybe she'd thought of someone to help with Puff. "Hi, Mrs. Murphy," she answered, smiling.

"Hi. Please call me Gwen. How's Puff?"

"She's doing really well. How about Marigold?"

"Fine. They think I'm overly worried about her, when I'm being a good cat mom."

"I understand. I'm glad she's okay. I haven't been able to find a cat sitter. Have you come up with someone?"

"Yes—me."

And just in the nick of time. A load dropped off Sarah's shoulders. "Really? That'd be great. Where do you live?"

Gwen gave Sarah her address, and wow. "You're just a few blocks from my house, close enough to walk."

"Is that so! What exactly do you need me to do, and how often?"

She was about to share the particulars when her phone signaled an incoming call from Daniel. "Hang on," she told Gwen, then quickly texted him. *Can't talk now. Will phone you back.*

As soon as she sent the text, she returned to Gwen. "I don't work weekends, so you won't have to do a thing till Monday. I'd rather give you the particulars in person. I leave for work really early in the morning. Is it possible for you to stop by tonight or sometime tomorrow? I'll show you where I hide the key then." She barely knew the woman and didn't want her to have access to the key except when she stopped by to feed Puff. She didn't have those qualms about handing a key to Daniel to hold on to because she knew he was honest and decent. Gwen probably was, too.

"Let's do it tonight. How about in thirty minutes?"

"Perfect."

As soon as they disconnected, she phoned Daniel. "Hey," he answered, in that slightly husky voice she so liked.

Her stomach went all fluttery, and she silently ordered herself to settle down. "Hey there. You won't believe what just happened." She told him about Gwen's offer to look in on Puff. "She'll be here in about half an hour so I can show her what to do, like I did you."

"I'll bet that's a relief. You don't have to spend your weekend trying to find someone."

"I'm stoked about it. Thanks for the updates on Puff. I appreciated them. And your family's coming for Thanksgiving. That's great news, huh?"

"I think so," He sounded uncertain.

"Oh?" She wanted to know why, but didn't feel comfortable asking just yet. Maybe if she talked about her situation, he'd do the same. "My father was a first-class jerk. He dumped my mother, my brother, and me, and found himself another woman."

"That sucks."

"It was hard on all of us. At first, my mom was a

basket case, mostly because he let her know he'd left on a voicemail while she was at work. But once he took off and she realized he'd done us a favor, life was much more peaceful. We left Portland and moved to Guff's Lake. She met her current husband here. Mason's a great guy and they're really happy. I'm not real close to either of them, but family is family, and I love them. My mother, brother, and Mason, anyway. We haven't heard from or seen my father since he left."

"Do you miss him?"

"I used to, but I'm fine now. If he doesn't want to see me, it's his loss." Daniel was quiet, so she went ahead and asked. "What's your story?"

The silence went on so long, she wondered if the line had gone dead. "Daniel? You there?"

He cleared his throat. "I'm thinking about what to tell you."

That was his choice. For a few seconds she felt hurt, but he wasn't a man who shared much about himself. "You don't have to say anything if you don't want to."

"It's not that. I never talk about this." Questions filled her head, but she held off and he went on. "After Kendall passed away, my family got weird. They were also grieving, of course, and sat with me at the funeral and had me over for meals. Then one day, they stopped mentioning her or the accident. I got a lot of pitying looks, but little else, like they'd put it all be-hind them."

That sounded devastating, and when he paused for a long moment, she imagined he was pulling him-self together. "Kendall and her death became a taboo subject for all of them, including my sister Izzy, and we were real close, and her husband, Cyrus. It felt like they were smothering me in pity and pretense and thought I should put it out of my mind."

Not a pretty story, and her heart ached for him. No wonder her sympathetic expression the other day had silenced him. She wished he was beside her and she could hug him. "That must've been awful."

"Hellish, with no end in sight. After a few months of that, I realized I needed to move away. I'd been hiking in Guff's Lake before and really liked the town. The Fire Department was hiring, and I applied and got the job. Settling down here is one of the best decisions I ever made. That's it."

"You haven't seen anyone in your family since?"

"No, and when we talk on the phone, they're still fakey happy with me, pretending everything's fine.

If you didn't count that he was alone and still grieving. Sarah was alone, too, by choice. In the past, she'd been way too hasty, falling into relationships that never lasted. The most recent disaster with Jensen had been the worst. Since then, she'd become more careful and hadn't had a date since he'd dumped her a year before she'd first laid eyes on Daniel. Now she was open to meeting guys and dating again, although so far, she hadn't met anyone she wanted to date except Daniel. Too bad he wasn't interested.

His willingness to share the pain he'd suffered made her feel closer to him, like their friendship had deepened. "Thanks for telling me. I won't say a word to anyone."

"I'd appreciate that. It's not a secret, but I'd rather people didn't know. I don't need anyone feeling sorry for me. Though I have to admit, talking to you and getting it off my chest is a good feeling."

Although she had no chance of anything beyond

friendship with him, her heart lifted. "I'm flattered you trusted me."

"You're easy to talk to and a great listener. Just be warned that when the family is here and I'm about to go nuts, I might reach out to you."

"I hope you will. Before I forget, good luck with that class on Tuesday."

"I'll make sure to look for your mom."

"She's psyched—can't wait to meet Mr. November in person. I doubt she's the only one." The doorbell chimed. "I have to go—Gwen's here."

Pleased Daniel had opened up, she answered the door smiling.

BETWEEN FIRES AND MEDICAL CALLS, Daniel and his crewmates spent a busy Monday at the firehouse, and time seemed to fly. With every dispatch call from Sarah, he thought of her. Same as he'd been doing for days now. His feelings for her were growing. Late morning, after fighting a fire that had started in a rickety garage piled with stacks of old newspapers, junk, and debris, he and Ethan tidied and prepped the engine for the next call. While they worked, his thoughts spilled out.

"I really like Sarah."

"So you mentioned at the poker game the other night. You said you were friends. Are you two moving beyond friendship already?"

"No idea." Daniel wasn't sure how he felt, but even if he suspected things might be headed that direction, he wasn't ready to admit it.

"Does she have a boyfriend?"

The thought jarred him. She hadn't mentioned anyone and didn't act like she did. "I doubt it."

"Maybe you should find out. If she doesn't, then go from there and spend time with her."

Feeling like the ignorant kid he'd once been, he scratched the back of his neck. "I know that, okay? Maybe I will, maybe I won't. Don't go getting any ideas."

"Hanging with a woman whose company you enjoy isn't a commitment—it's a way to get to know her better. No harm in that." Ethan's stomach growled, and he checked his watch. "It's lunchtime. Let's eat."

They'd barely finished when another call came in. A grease fire in the kitchen had flared up and the female living there hadn't been able to put it out. Luckily and with minimal damage, the team quickly doused it. The rest of the afternoon was quiet, and Daniel and several teammates worked out in the gym.

Early that evening, a call sent him and several crewmates to an apartment across town, where an inebriated male had broken a bottle of bourbon and badly sliced his hand. After dressing the wound, they dropped him at the ER for further care. Back in the firehouse, dead on his feet, he fell into bed.

8

After breakfast Tuesday morning, Daniel gathered his training kit and headed for the Massage Plush Spa at Guff's Lake Resort to teach the hour-long emergency preparedness class. He was primed and ready to share valuable information with the group.

The class was in a meeting room off the spa. They were a small group—six massage therapists, four receptionists, and several other employees who sold merchandise and otherwise worked near the customers and spa staff. Roughly a quarter of the participants were male, the rest female. They didn't look too excited about sitting through a boring class, but he planned to change that. At the start, he introduced himself and invited them to do the same. As they went around the room, he recognized Sarah's mom before she said a word. Her name was Lee Ferguson, and Sarah looked a lot like her—same blonde hair and wide smile. Sarah was prettier, though.

He started off talking about the garage fire mishap the previous day, and added another tale about a couple whose heater short-circuited, causing a fire, smoke damage, and a trip to the hospital. Real situations Sarah had encouraged him to share as they'd reviewed the training materials. He followed with a question she'd suggested. "How could these mishaps have been prevented?"

Hands raised and a good conversation ensued. In no time, the group was engaged and interested, offering comments and posing questions. When that petered out, he questioned them about clients who'd suffered sudden medical issues on the massage table and asked them to share what'd happened. There weren't many of those, but it led to a discussion about what to do in an emergency. He explained that all firefighters at the fire station were trained EMTs, and suggested additional training classes they might want to take.

The session ran late, but he didn't mind. When it ended, the majority of attendees went back to work. Those who weren't scheduled lingered behind to chat. Lee was one of them. "I hear you know my daughter, Sarah," she said, when the room had emptied and he was packing up his stuff.

Wondering what Sarah had told her, he flashed a smile. "We firefighters depend on her. She's steered us through many an emergency."

Lee beamed at him. "That does my heart proud. When you rescued the kitten...well, you really impressed her."

Nice hearing that. "It was my day off and my good deed for the day." He checked his watch. "I have to get back to the station. Glad you enjoyed the class."

"If you see Sarah, tell her hi."

It'd been a week since they'd last seen each other, but okay. "We don't work in the same building, but I'll let her know." He looked forward to that. It'd be fun to talk about meeting her mom. He also wanted to get her a thank-you gift for helping him prep for what'd been a successful class. Maybe he'd stop by her place tomorrow, the day she was off. She might be out, but it couldn't hurt to try. They were friends, so why not?

When he didn't have a photo of Kendall handy to talk to, he communicated with her in his mind. This usually helped him cope with whatever happened to bother him. It wasn't something he told people—talking to his dead wife in his head or to a photo of her? They'd think he was nuts. "I like this woman," he mentally confessed. "But don't worry, you're number one in my heart and always will be." Conscience assuaged, he went back to thinking about Sarah. Maybe he'd screw up his nerve and invite her to dinner sometime. He looked forward to that way too much.

BP—BEFORE Puff—Sarah slept in on Wednesdays and weekends, but the kitten wanted her breakfast bright and early. That morning being a Wednesday, Puff didn't stir until five a.m., which was better than four. The little stinker made up for allowing her the extra hour of sleep by meowing loudly. Loud enough that Erin woke up, too. She padded out of her bedroom, yawning. "I can't wait until Puff is big enough to sleep in, or at least use an automatic feeder to feed herself."

"That'll be great—if she likes dry food. At least she's eating, right? She's growing by the day. On the plus side, you and I can have breakfast together before you leave." A rare occurrence with their schedules.

While Erin showered and got ready for work, Sarah let the demanding kitten out of her sleeping cage and fed her. Then she made coffee.

Erin emerged from the bathroom dressed in business casual pants and a blazer, her hair framing her face in a way Sarah envied. "I love that hair style. I wish my hair was thicker and straighter so I could wear mine that way."

"In case you don't know this, the natural waves in your hair are killer," Erin said, as they ate and guzzled coffee strong enough to perk them up. "What's on your agenda today?"

"After I laze around in my pj's for a while, I'll take a leisurely shower. Then knitting, of course, if I can keep Puff away from the yarn—I have a lot left to do before the holiday craft fair opens. It's a good thing she naps so much. When I get tired of that, whatever I feel like doing. I've been craving chocolate chip cookies, so I might make a batch from scratch. And of course, I'll play with Puff."

"A whole day to do what you want—I envy that."

"Hey, you get to sleep later than I do in the morning."

"When I remember to drown out Puff's meowing with white noise. I forgot to turn it on last night. Which reminds me—I'll be staying at Flick's tonight."

"That makes twice this week, and we're only on Wednesday. You two are getting serious."

"We are." Erin wore a dreamy look. "I'm in love."

"And he loves you back. Must be nice."

"Mmm hmm. How's Daniel?"

"Fine, I guess." Sarah hadn't seen him in a week, and they hadn't talked since Sunday. He didn't think about her much, she guessed, which was to be expected. She propped her chin on her fist and wished he'd get in touch.

"By the longing look on your face, it's obvious you like him more than ever."

"Unfortunately. Too bad it's one-sided."

Her friend gave a sympathetic nod. "You know, you don't have to wait for him to make a move."

"I'm not comfortable with that, remember?" Erin didn't know about the tragedy in his life, and Sarah wasn't about to fill her in. "I guarantee, that wouldn't work."

Erin glanced at her watch and stood. "I wish we could talk more, but I'd better go or I'll be late."

While Sarah played with Puff and knitted away while she napped, she daydreamed about Daniel. A useless waste of her brain, and she firmly pushed all thoughts of him away.

She was finally ready to shower and get dressed when the doorbell rang. Must be a delivery with something Erin had ordered online. She peered through the peephole in the door and saw Daniel. And her still in her robe and pj's. She hadn't even brushed her hair.

After a quick finger-combing, she tightened the sash of her robe and scooped up Puff so she didn't escape out the door. Then she opened it.

9

———————

Daniel was surprised to find Sarah in a robe and slippers, as if she'd just gotten out of bed. And it was midmorning. She looked cute but embarrassed to see him. Feeling like a jerk, he cleared his throat. "I didn't take you for a late riser. I should've called first."

"Actually, thanks to Puff the alarm clock princess, I've been up for hours." With a slight frown, she glanced down at herself and pulled the lapels of her robe closer together. "I'm lazy today and as you can see, I haven't gotten around to getting dressed. Wish I had. What brings you here?"

Uncertain what to say, he wiped his boots on the welcome mat. "Invite me in, and I'll tell you. It's cold outside."

He'd barely ditched his parka when Puff made a beeline for him and started to climb up one leg of his jeans. Her claws were too little to do any harm, but strong enough that she had no trouble scaling his leg. Grinning, he cupped her in his hand. "Hey there, Puff. Since I last saw you, you've grown. You seem to be thriving."

"She's doing so well." Sarah's smile lit up the room.

"She's put on weight and is more playful every day. I took her in earlier for her shots and set up an appointment to get her spayed. The date for that is next Wednesday."

"If I were you, I'd wouldn't tell her." He winked. "I take it Erin's okay with having a kitten in the house."

"As it turns out, she loves Puff as much as I do. How could she not?" Sarah paused. "I don't think she'll be around much longer, though. She and her boyfriend are getting pretty serious. It's only a matter of time before they move in together."

"Seems to be a hot trend right now. Several guys at the firehouse are in similar positions. Will her leaving bother you?"

"A little of both. She's my closest friend, and I'll miss her. But at the same time, I'm happy she found love with a wonderful guy."

Daniel nodded and hoped things worked out better than they had for him. "Your purring is louder, too, Puff." Sarah was studying the two of them with undisguised warmth that felt good. "What are you staring at?"

"You're so big, and she's so little, and the size difference doesn't seem to faze her at all. I wish I were that fearless."

"You seem strong to me. You're not easily rattled, either. Handling rough calls from panicky people and smoothly directing emergency response teams to the rescue takes a coolness and grit most people don't have." Her gratified expression warmed him inside in ways he didn't understand. Had no one complimented her on her work before?

"Thanks, Daniel. I never thought of myself that way. Puff's really got a thing for you. Would you mind if I took a photo?"

"Why not? She already knows I'm a sucker for her. Just don't tell Toad. Hold this, will ya?" He handed her the bag he'd picked up on the way over.

"Okay." She eyed the red, black, and gold Rosemary's Breakfast Nook logo and licked her lips. "Even seeing that label makes my mouth water." She set it down on a chair, then snapped several photos and sent them to him. "I appreciate the treat, but you haven't said what you're doing here."

"Well—" Oddly on edge, he pulled at the open collar of his flannel shirt. "We're both off today, and I don't have any detailing jobs scheduled. Figured I'd stop by and bring you a little something." He nodded toward the sack. "Go for it."

She raised the bag and sniffed the thing before peering inside. "Oh, man, are those cookies?"

"Samantha's oatmeal with chocolate chunks, a thank-you for prepping me with great ideas for teaching that class."

Sarah licked her lips. "Everything Sam makes is delicious. But you didn't have to do this. You treated me to breakfast and looked in on Puff and fed her twice. That's thanks enough."

"Then you don't want these cookies?" he teased.

Laughing, she held tightly to the bag. "I didn't say that. The truth is, lately I've been craving chocolate chip cookies. I was planning to make some this afternoon, and now I don't have to. I could kiss you!" Her cheeks went scarlet, and she quickly added, "It's a figure of speech, so don't worry—I won't."

"Okay." Although he wouldn't have minded. The thought should've filled him with guilt, but didn't. Grateful for the reprieve, he got serious about asking her to dinner and going from there.

"How about this instead?" She smacked her lips with such anticipation, he chuckled.

"You're cute, know that?" Out of the blue, the urge to kiss her hit him hard. Blame her for using the figure of speech. Not exactly. The truth was, he'd been thinking about it for days. Better not go there. He pushed the urge away.

"Me, cute? I haven't even combed my hair yet." She muttered something about showering and dressing.

"Hey, if you want to clean up and get dressed, I don't mind. As long as you share those cookies with me. Just one—the rest are yours."

"I'm happy to share. After I get dressed, I want to hear about that class. I made a big pot of coffee earlier, and there's plenty left. Why don't I heat it up? Then we'll sit down at the kitchen table and eat cookies while you tell me about the class." She glanced at the kitten, who was sleeping blissfully. "You don't have to hold her. She'll probably curl up someplace and finish napping."

"I don't mind."

"Up to you. Make yourself comfortable—I'll be right back." She disappeared down the hall.

"I really like her," he told Puff. "But there's really nothing between us," he added for his own sake. "Think she'll hang out with me?" The kitten woke up and jumped out of his hand. "Guess I know how you feel about that. You don't have to worry—I'll behave."

When Sarah returned, she'd pulled her hair back and changed into a burgundy pullover sweater that hugged her breasts and a pair of snug-fitting jeans she looked good in. Make that *great*. Damn, she was attractive.

"I feel better now," she said.

"That was quick. Tell me where you keep the mugs and I'll pour the coffee."

"You do that and I'll set the cookies out. Mugs are in the cabinet over the kitchen counter."

He watched her walk away, toward the living room where she'd left the bag, her hips swaying seductively. His body stirred and he silently swore for getting ahead of himself. After so much time alone, he was seriously out of practice. They were friends, nothing more, he reminded himself, so all was good.

Moments later, bag in hand, she joined him at the table. She sipped her coffee, bit into a cookie, and murmured in pleasure. "This is delicious. I want to hear about the class."

"It was great. People seemed to enjoy it. They asked good questions, too. The hour flew by, and we ran a little over. Afterward, your mom came over to thank me. She's nice."

"Was she interested in what you had to say?"

"Definitely. I'm supposed to say 'hi' from her, but I'm sure she told you about that."

"I hadn't heard."

"She didn't phone you after the class?"

Sarah shook her head. "Lee and I are both busy and don't talk that much. I can only take personal calls at work when I'm on break."

She'd mentioned they weren't close. "You call her Lee?"

"Not to her face. My brother Elton and I both do."

Interesting. "Speaking of busy, things were crazy at the station yesterday. But you know that."

"Don't I, though. My shift was ending when the elderly man fell and couldn't get up, and his wife was unable to help him—how did that go?"

"He wasn't sure why he fell, but he checked out

okay. To be on the safe side, we suggested he see his doctor."

"I hope he follows through."

"The last time you and I talked, Mrs. Murphy was coming over to meet Puff and learn where to find the cat stuff. How'd that go?"

"For starters, she asked me to call her Gwen. I like her. She's friendly and seems eager to help out." The way Sarah had always longed for her mother to be. "I think she enjoyed it, too. She offered to come over again this week. She's retired and has the time, plus she lives just a few blocks from here. Depending on what happens after Puff gets spayed, it'll only be for a week or so. By then, she won't have to eat so often, and I won't have to worry about finding anyone else to look in on her."

This was good news. "You lucked out with Mrs. Murphy—er, Gwen."

"Right?"

Relief and happiness lit up her face. She sure was pretty. He liked her maybe more than he'd thought. In the moments of silence between them, he battled with himself about inviting her to dinner.

She squinted at him. "What's with the confused expression?"

How to explain without misleading her? Stalling for time, he gulped coffee and decided to find out. "I need to ask you something."

"Okay." She fiddled with the handle of her mug as if worried.

He opened his mouth to tell her he wanted to go out together just for fun, but ended up blurting something he hadn't intended to admit. "I really like being with you, Sarah, and I'd like to see more of you. I don't know if you're interested or not. Heck, maybe you're involved with someone. Plus, I come with a lot of baggage."

For a long moment she was silent. Then, "Sounds to me like you're trying to talk me out of wanting to get to know you better."

It wasn't a rejection, and he straightened his shoulders. "Not at all. Just warning you who I am."

"I know you're an honest, kind, good man and a brave firefighter, and that you miss your wife. Anyway, we all have baggage."

He was curious about hers. "You know about mine. Your turn."

She caught her lush bottom lip between her teeth, and the urge to kiss her grew stronger. Somehow he buried it and waited for what she had to say. "Before I answer that, you should know that I don't have a boyfriend, mainly because I've had my share of rotten relationships. I'm not the best judge of men. That's the baggage part."

"Go on," he encouraged, interested in finding out more.

"You really want to know?" He nodded, and she went on. "My most recent relationship ended just shy of six months together before Jensen—that's his name —dumped me. By text, after he left my house one night, if you can believe that." Her lips curled in a sneer. "Then he ghosted me. Later, I visited his social media accounts and found out he had a new girlfriend. I believe they're engaged now."

"Ouch. Jensen sounds like a real piece of work."

"A jerk and a coward. I should've guessed—there were plenty of signs. Canceled plans, failure to show up without any explanation, stuff like that. Crazy me gave him a pass almost every time because I wanted things to work out." She glanced down at her mug. "In hindsight, I'm glad he left. I haven't dated since, by choice."

"I hear that. About a year back, I tried my hand at dating. Nothing serious, just wanted someone to hang with. I ended up taking out two different women. Neither date worked out." Understatement of the year. One had thrown herself at him and begged him for sex. The other had blatantly admitted she wanted to marry him. No, thanks. He grimaced.

"That's obvious from your frown." She angled her head and did a little frowning herself. "Is this your roundabout way of saying you want to go out with me?"

It was, he realized. "We're both out of practice, but yeah. It'll be fun."

"I could use some fun. For all you know, I could be a terrible date, too."

"I doubt that. So far, we've had a great time together. If all goes well, we still will. But I don't want to be one of those guys who hurts you. So I'll say up front that I'm not looking for anything serious." He wasn't even close to wanting that, and wouldn't for a long time, if at all.

"I'm with you on that." She glanced down a moment before going on, as if thinking, or maybe holding something back. Instinct told him the latter, but he wasn't about to press her about it. "I don't know about dating, but I'm willing to spend time with you so we can find out more about each other," she added. "That way, there's no pressure on either of us. Does that work for you?" She finished with slightly pursed lips.

Did she have to have such an enticing mouth? The need to kiss her, even more powerful than before, almost overwhelmed him. Bad idea and way too soon.

Shoving the urge away, he focused on the conversation instead of his misguided attraction. "Heck, yeah."

"All right," she said, and they high-fived across the table. "As far as spending time together, what do you have in mind?"

Besides wanting to taste that mouth? "Why don't we have dinner tonight? Unless it's too short notice."

"I don't have any plans, so that works. It won't be a late night, though. I'll be getting up tomorrow morning at four and need to get to bed early."

"Not a problem. What kind of food do you like?"

"Pretty much anything. Marv's would be great. Their pies are so good."

Daniel was on board with that. "I like that place, too. If I pick you up around five-fifteen, we'll beat most of the crowd. I'll have you home in plenty of time to get that full night's sleep."

"Then I'll see you in a few hours."

That'd worked out well, and he whistled as he left.

~

DINNER WITH DANIEL! Sarah squealed with excitement. He had no idea how long she'd fantasized about this, or that she'd fibbed about the 'getting serious' thing. He'd freak for sure if he found out she'd had a major crush on him way before he'd noticed her. Something he'd never know. More often than not, her tendency to jump into things way too quickly ended in disaster. The worst being with Jensen.

She'd mentioned the breakup to Daniel, but had neglected to share the humiliating details. Now, they flooded into her mind. After having sex one night, she'd sensed him pulling away. Out of desperation to hold his interest, she'd blurted out that she loved him.

His less-than-thrilled expression and the snort that followed had burned a hole in her fragile self-esteem, a bad memory she'd never forget. "I didn't sign up for this," he'd said, while stepping into his jeans and pulling his shirt over his head.

Genuinely puzzled, she'd frowned. "What are you talking about?"

"I don't love you and never have."

"You sure acted like you did."

"Then you misunderstood."

"Can we talk about this, maybe work things out?" she said, hating her pleading tone.

"There's nothing to say."

Much later that evening, after she'd fallen asleep, he'd texted that they were over. She still shuddered at the way she'd shamed herself as the neediest fool ever, begging him not to go. But she'd learned her lesson—never tell a man she loved him unless he said the words first. And forget pitiful begging. She'd moved on, and good riddance.

Go slowly, that was her mantra now and would help her keep her head on straight. With that, she went back to thinking about the evening ahead. Daniel didn't want to get serious, but at least she knew it and was going into whatever this thing they shared was with her eyes open. If she were smart, she'd contact him and change her mind, but she wanted to go out with him. As long as she held onto her heart, which she would. Or so she assured herself. Bursting to share the news with Erin, she texted. *Going out with Daniel tonight!*

Busy at work, her friend sent a heart emoji.

After knitting and playing with Puff that afternoon, she culled through her closet for something to wear. Nothing dressy—Marv's was a blue-collar diner

—but something she looked good in. After a brief search, she settled on two-inch-heeled leather boots, winter-white corduroy pants that flattered her hips and made her legs look longer than they were, and a sapphire pullover that brought out the green flecks in her eyes. She left her hair down, securing it with tortoise shell clips. Minimal makeup—a brush of color on her cheeks, mascara, and a touch of lip gloss.

Done. With Puff in hand, she studied herself in the full-length mirror a previous tenant had attached to the bathroom door. "What do you think, Puff? Do I look good?"

Paying her no attention, the kitten meowed and jumped down as if saying, "How the heck would I know? I'm a cat, remember? Now, feed me."

Soon after she added food to Puff's bowl, the doorbell rang. Daniel had arrived. Forcing herself to walk slowly when she wanted to hurry and let him in, she made her way to the door. "Hi," she greeted, and gestured him inside. "You're right on time."

"Punctuality has been ingrained in me since I was a kid." His gaze flicked over her. "You look great."

"Thanks." She noted the black jeans and slate turtleneck under his black leather jacket. "So do you." She swore he blushed. She'd had no idea the big man did that and was charmed.

"Hey, Puff." The kitten briefly glanced his way before returning to her dinner. "You sure have a healthy appetite." His attention returned to Sarah. "Ready?"

She nodded. "Bye, Puff. Be good."

Marv's was on the south side of town, a good fifteen-minute drive. The sun was sinking fast. "Every day seems to get dark earlier," she said.

"Happens every winter. Is it warm enough in here?"

"I'm nice and cozy."

On the drive they chit-chatted. Daniel told her about the BMW he'd detailed. "She's a sweet car with pretty metallic bronze paint. I took a photo." At a red light, he handed her his phone to see.

"I love that color."

"What'd you do after I left this afternoon?" he asked, lifting his hip up and tucking the phone into his back pocket.

"Played with Puff, knitted, then knitted some more."

"I assume making hats and scarves."

"You win the prize for guessing right. All shapes, colors, and sizes."

He slowed down and turned into the parking area. It was early yet, but a good deal of the slots were filled. "So much for beating the crowd."

He came around the car as she opened her door. As she slid out, she caught a whiff of his clean, fresh, masculine scent. She wanted to lean in closer and inhale it, but didn't.

"Even from out here, the food smells good," he said, as they neared the entrance. "My stomach is rumbling."

"I'm hungry, too." Between the country music pouring from the old juke-box, the buzz of conversation, and the clatter of dishes, the place was as noisy as always. Surrounded by the aromas of good food, she salivated and glanced around. "Most of the tables are taken."

"I see an empty one for two over there, in the corner."

He put his hand on her lower back and started forward. A harmless gesture that nevertheless added a joyous bump to her heart.

As they headed for the table, she noticed familiar faces. "Cherry and Mary Jo, two friends from the dispatch center, are to your left over there," she said, in a loud enough voice for Daniel to hear over the din. They were the only people besides Erin who knew about her crush. "Mind if I say hello?"

"Not at all." The two women, both married and older than Sarah, stared at him. "I'm sure you recognize Daniel O'Dwyer," she said, and introduced her friends.

Both women nodded, and Mary Jo, who was pushing forty, beamed at him. "It's wonderful to meet you in person, Mr. November."

Not to be outdone, Cherry, in her early-thirties, placed her hand over her heart. "I have two autographed copies of the calendar—one in my kitchen and the other near my desk at dispatch. It's so cool that you and your teammates signed them."

He flashed a smile. "Thanks for supporting us. Pleasure meeting you both." Leaning in a fraction, he touched Sarah's shoulder. "We should snag that table while we can."

"Right. See you tomorrow," she told her friends, knowing they'd expect a full report.

"I've never met anyone you work with," he said, as they made their way to the back corner. "They must dispatch for other districts."

"That's right. They're two of my favorites."

"They sure looked us over. I wonder what they were thinking."

"Probably curious how I got lucky enough to be here with you. You're a minor celebrity, you know."

"So people think."

"Does that bother you?"

"It's getting old, but in about six weeks a new calendar with guys on a different shift comes out. Then my so-called celebrity will fade into the past. But I really don't mind that. Thanks to the calendar, we raised a great deal of money for the benefit fund. It's helped a lot of people who lost their homes to fires."

Soon after they draped their coats over the backs of their seats and sat down, one of his knees bumped hers. "Sorry," he said. "My legs are pretty long—but you found that out at our breakfast meeting."

"I don't mind." Mind? The brief connection set off all sorts of tingles. The door opened, and more familiar faces tromped into the room. "Liam, Tony, and Nate just walked through the door, and they're coming this way."

Daniel glanced over his shoulder. "So I see." He gave a pained look and muttered something under his breath.

The three men greeted her and turned mischievous grins toward Daniel, as if they knew something she didn't. What she *did* know was that being surrounded by four gorgeous males was a real treat.

"Why don't you two move to a bigger table and we'll eat together?" Liam asked.

Daniel shook his head. "Another time."

"No worries. See you at the next poker game."

The men moved off to find their own table. "Why were they grinning like Cheshire cats?" she asked, as they ambled off.

"They caught me on a date with you," he grumbled.

He seemed unhappy about that, and Sarah took offense. "If you're embarrassed to be seen with me..."

The second the words were out, his brow furrowed. "What gave you that idea? I'm proud to be here with you." His eyes lit up, making her feel sexy.

She melted a little. "Really?"

"Absolutely. But those guys are a nosy bunch. Before long, everyone at the firehouse will know we had dinner together."

"It'll be the same with Cherry, Mary Jo, and other people at the dispatch center. Let them talk—what do we care?" she said, although she couldn't wait to share every detail.

A male server stopped at the table and took their orders. The conversation continued. "Even if we did run into people we know, I'm glad we chose this diner," she added. "I haven't been in ages."

"So that's why I've never seen you here."

"Then you come often?"

"Several times a year."

"When I think of all the pies you've eaten...I'm jealous and am so looking forward to a fat slice of coconut cream pie."

His lips quirked. "If you weren't, I'd be surprised. You have quite the sweet tooth."

"What makes you say that?"

"Cookies earlier, pie tonight...It's obvious."

"You found me out." She wasn't going to add that she also had a sweet tooth for him—a big one. "I'm not the only one. You like sugary things, too."

"I can't deny that." The look on his face when he glanced briefly at her mouth made her yearn for a kiss.

The meal was tasty and the talk easy. Daniel wanted to know how she'd gotten into knitting. "Lee's pretty high-strung and the anxiety was contagious," she explained. "In high school, I signed up for an after-school knitting class. Sitting quietly, turning yarn into wonderful things, relaxes me. How did you get into car detailing?"

"I needed something to do when I wasn't on shift. Rob started the company, and it grew too big for him to handle by himself. It's still growing. He needed someone to help out. That's how it started. We're talking about me becoming a partner in the business."

"Cool."

"I think so." He paused. "This may sound weird, but I get a charge from cleaning up a dirty vehicle."

"That doesn't sound weird at all. It's good you found something you enjoy."

The meal over, they ordered dessert. He wanted lemon pie, and she had the coconut cream she'd mentioned. She tasted his, he tasted hers. Laughing, they argued over whose was better. In the end, they agreed both were excellent. By the time they finished the meal and put their coats on to leave, Sarah's friends had gone. The firefighters were still there, enjoying themselves and sharing a pitcher.

"Leaving so soon?" Hank called out as they passed that table.

He nodded. "Gotta get Sarah home. She'll be up at four to get ready for her shift."

As he had earlier, he touched her back with his hand and guided her out. There and then, she wanted to melt into his arms. *Slow down,* she silently warned and pulled herself together.

10

"That was fun," Sarah said, as Daniel unlocked his car.

"I enjoyed it, too." He glanced over at her and the urge to plant a kiss on those lips about killed him. Somehow, he managed to behave himself.

"I hope your firefighter friends don't bug you too much about me," she added.

"I'm sure they will. They're like family, and that means at times they can be hard to take."

"So true. Speaking of family, have you found a place for Thanksgiving dinner?"

He groaned. "With six people plus me and on such short notice, it's not so easy. What are your plans?"

"I'll be at Lee and Mason's with my brother Elton."

"Nice that you have a place to go." He envied her that.

She made a so-so gesture with her hand. "Elton has a busy social life, and I know he'll leave early. Then it'll be just me, Lee, and Mason."

"On a holiday, and all of you full and happy? It can't be that bad."

"You're right about the good food, and I love Lee

and Mason, but they'll be on me about my love life. Especially Lee. She's decided it's time for me to meet someone, settle down, and give her grandchildren. Mason likes the idea, too, but he leaves the nagging to her. It gets tiring."

Daniel sympathized. "They sound like my parents. They can't bring up Kendall, but they have no problem pushing me to get out and meet someone, no matter how often I tell them to back off."

"They don't always listen," Sarah said, and shook her head.

They buckled in and he headed off into the night, the street lights along the road guiding the way. Not much traffic, either. After that, neither of them said much until Sarah broke the silence just as he turned onto her street. "They mean well, though. Right or wrong, they think they know what's best for us."

"Yeah, and that got old, like yesterday." As he pulled up in front of the house, his phone pinged with a message. He checked it and couldn't stop a grin. "Looks like my family and I have a place to eat Thanksgiving dinner."

"That's great. Where?"

"The Hearthstone at the Guff's Lake Resort."

"Wow. Have you eaten there?" He shook his head and she continued. "It's a place people go for special occasions, and the food is excellent. I can't believe they have a table at this late date. How did you manage that?"

"The people who work there have a thing for firefighters. Also, the reservation is for one o'clock in the afternoon instead of later. Do you mind waiting while I text them a big ol' thank you?"

"Not at all."

Moments later, he put his phone away. "It's great to have that settled."

"So your smile tells me. Your family will love the experience. After the meal, they may want to walk around the resort."

"I'll likely show them around before then. Either way, they'll be impressed. It should be a good time for us all. I'll let them know tomorrow." He put all that aside and focused on the beautiful woman in the passenger seat. Something had happened to her hair. "Check your hair on the left side."

"Oh?" She felt around with her fingers and frowned. "I can't believe this. The hair clip on that side is gone. How did I not know that? Darn it, it was tortoiseshell, my favorite one."

Distracted by the unhappy pucker of her lips, he scooted to the edge of his seat, reached across the bucket seat, and tucked the wayward hunk of hair behind her ear. Of its own accord, his hand lingered there. Her skin was soft, and she smelled sweet. She went very still, her eyes locked on his. The longing he saw there zapped any hold on his self-control. He had to taste those lips, *had* to. "Hey, Sarah."

She swallowed visibly. "Yes, Daniel?"

He shut off the engine, exited the RAV4, and walked around to the passenger side. She was already out of the car, same as when he'd parked at Marv's.

"What are you doing?" she asked.

Spellbound by that mouth, he forced his gaze higher. "Walking you to your door."

"That's not necessary, but if you insist..."

He held out his hand and she took it. "I had a great time tonight," he said, when she'd unlocked it.

"Me, too."

The longing look had returned, and he decided to go for it. "This may be out of line, but I really want to kiss you." He caught his breath and waited for her to refuse.

Instead, she reached for him. "I've been wanting that since we had breakfast the other day."

~

SARAH COULD HARDLY BELIEVE she was in Daniel's arms, kissing him on the front step on a cold, dark night. At five-feet-seven in bare feet plus the added height from her ankle boots, she wasn't short, but he was a good six or seven inches taller and had to bend down to kiss her. Both of them in heavy coats that prevented any real body contact. It wasn't nearly enough. *Move slowly*, she reminded herself. *I will*, she silently promised, taking his hand. "Come inside."

Almost in unison, they shed their coats. Then he kissed her again. This time, he cupped her waist in his big, warm hands—how could they be so warm when hers were ice cold?—and lifted her up as if she weighed nothing. She felt the heat of his body, his solid chest and strong arms. Much more satisfying. With a sigh, she hugged him closer and responded with a more serious kiss.

He let out a groan and eagerly participated. The kisses that followed, lots of them, grew steadily deeper until his tongue was in her mouth. It seemed forever since she'd been kissed, and never like this. In no time, she jumped from mild arousal to steaming hot lust. The mantra to slow down faded into oblivion.

Suddenly, Puff began to climb the leg of her cords, a distraction and a blessing—she'd wanted too much, way too quickly. She pulled out of his arms. "Look who decided to visit. I've got to teach her not to climb on me."

"If that's possible. Well, hello there," Daniel said. "At least her claws don't hurt much. Yet." They both gave her their attention before she jumped to the floor and sauntered off. "That got pretty intense," he added, and again brushed the stubborn lock of hair back.

"Surprisingly so." His hot eyes and tender touch filled her with longing to walk back into his arms. But she wasn't about to do that. Ready for him to leave before she got herself into trouble, she plucked their coats from the floor and handed him his. She pulled hers to her chest, as if it could shield her from him.

"That's right, you need your beauty sleep."

"I do." Although she was nowhere near ready to fall asleep. Too much to think about. "Thanks for tonight," she added, as she walked him to the door. "I haven't had an evening like this in ages."

"I enjoyed it, too." He looked like he wanted to kiss her again, but refrained. "I'll be in touch."

After placing Puff in her sleep cage, she got ready for bed and thought about him stopping by that morning and the entire wonderful day that had ended with dinner and such delicious kisses. She liked him more than ever and wanted this to be the beginning of a romantic relationship with him, but face it, his heart belonged to his deceased wife. For all she knew, it always would. Regardless, he wasn't ready for what she wanted and might never be.

He'd warned her he didn't want to get serious, but she so did. The knowledge didn't stop her from wanting him, from forgetting to move slowly. What was she supposed to do about that? She knew the answer—avoid him and get over the intense feelings he'd likely never return. With her long hours at the dispatch center, steering clear wouldn't be difficult. It was the safest option. The only one.

In bed, she clutched her pillow and wished he were beside her.

11

That same night, Daniel lay in bed swearing up and down for letting his desire for Sarah take charge earlier. She'd felt so sweet in his arms, had given him a glimpse into passion he'd never suspected. It'd been a long time since he'd felt such hunger. Plain and simple, he wanted her. He turned on the bedside lamp, glanced at the photo of Kendall on the dresser across the room, and confessed. "I've been celibate for so long. I kissed Sarah tonight. I liked it. I like her."

Of course, she didn't answer, but he sensed something different. Like before, no guilt followed. Huh. He switched the light off.

That didn't mean he wanted anything serious. He knew Sarah was into him, but didn't want to lead her on and hurt her. Steering clear of her from now on was best for them both. His brain agreed, but the battle between it and his hungry body was relentless, and he spent much of the night tossing and turning. Sensing his torment, Toad whined in sympathy.

Muttering, Daniel got up. If it hadn't been pitch dark and pouring outside, he'd have gone out running to calm his restlessness. Instead, he paced his little apartment, his dog following him around with an he's-at-it-again look.

Sometime before morning, he climbed back into bed and slept. The alarm woke him at nine—he'd agreed to take care of a car detail Rob had scheduled for himself. Lately, he'd called on Daniel to do that often. No complaints there—the money was good, and his attention would be focused on the job instead of fantasizing about Sarah.

Time would tell if it worked.

THE FOLLOWING MORNING, Sarah showed up at the dispatch center still upset with herself for rushing into things with Daniel. Both Mary Jo and Cherry greeted her with expectant expressions. "We need details," Mary Jo said.

As much as she wanted to tell them what'd happened, they didn't need to know about the longing that'd almost derailed her plan to move slowly. Instead, she summarized. "We had a good time. He's a great kisser."

Both friends almost swooned. "Be careful," Mary Jo cautioned. "I'm sure there are of lots women after him." The dispatch buzzer rang, alerting everyone in the building that it was time to get to work.

The day was busy, too much so to think about her friend's warning or the previous evening. But during breaks and lunch, she thought about it a lot. She'd always known women were attracted to Daniel, but when they were together, she forgot. Besides, he seemed to like her, and his kisses reflected as much, although being a guy, that was only natural. She should never have invited him in.

That evening, Erin slept at the house. "We haven't spent much time together lately, and I'm dying to know," she said. "How was dinner with Daniel last night?"

"Fun. We ran into Cherry and Mary Jo from the dispatch center and also several of his teammates from the station. They invited us to sit with them, but he told them he wanted to eat alone with me—a dream come true! We get along really well, as if we've known each other for ages. It was special. And scary." She chewed a nail, which wasn't at all like her.

Erin eyed her. "What happened?"

"When we got to my house, he kissed me at the door. I should've stopped him there. Instead, I invited him in."

"Go on."

"We kissed a lot, and it was wonderful. The trouble was, things got hot pretty fast, and I forgot about moving slowly."

All ears, her bestie leaned toward her. "Did anything else happen?"

"Only what I told you. That's it."

"Then I don't see the problem. You're too hard on yourself. You didn't move as slowly as you wanted, but you didn't go any further than kissing. That counts as something."

"You know me—when I jump into things so quickly, my common sense disappears." Erin had held Sarah's hand through most of her failed relationships. "I thought sure I'd learned my lesson with Jensen and wouldn't rush into anything ever again. Why didn't I stick to my plan?" No matter how much she wanted Daniel. The flush of joy at the beginning of a relationship never lasted beyond a month or two—with the exception of her most recent relationship with Jensen

—and the after-effects were always painful, even when she initiated the breakup.

"I understand about getting involved so fast. It was that way with Flick and me. Sometimes you can't slow down."

"A big help you are."

"You're a strong woman. If you really want to move slowly, you will. Have faith in yourself. On a different note, it's about time Daniel noticed you."

"Sure, he likes me. But he's said more than once he doesn't want to get serious."

"He treated you to dinner, and those kisses are a positive sign. None of it would've happened if he wasn't interested."

"Interest is good, but I want more. At work today, Mary Jo reminded me of what I knew but had forgotten. Daniel's a sexy man plenty of women want for themselves. Even if he's interested in me now in a physical sense, it's a fact that sooner or later, he'll move on. And another thing—he's still carrying a torch for his dead wife." Stating the obvious wasn't a betrayal of what he'd confided to her.

"A fact? I don't think so. He might still be grieving for her, and who can blame him, but that doesn't mean he can't have feelings for you that could develop into something serious even if he doesn't think he wants that. You need a shot of confidence. You're beautiful and smart and fun, and he's finally realizing it, so quit wasting your time on doom and gloom. He's not Jensen, and thank the Universe for that. The guy was a train wreck."

What Erin said boosted her morale. "I needed to hear that. Thanks."

"Then show me some of that moxie you have and

brighten up. Let's talk about Puff. Where is she, anyway?"

At the mention of her name, the kitten pranced toward them. After they both greeted her, she yawned and headed toward her sleep cage.

"I saw that you scheduled her spay appointment," Erin said.

Sarah nodded. "Next Wednesday."

"There's a pamphlet you'll want to read about after-care for her. I'll send you a link with a list of things you'll need to pick up, including a kitty onesie to keep her from licking her wound. It's a no-no and could mess with the stitches."

Imagining the kitten unable to groom herself, Sarah frowned. "That sounds awful."

"It is, but she'll heal fast. Then you can toss it. Anyway, I'll bring a pamphlet home for you tomorrow. If you can bring her in for the appointment, I'll take her home after work the following afternoon."

"That'd be great. You're the best."

Erin was quiet a moment. Then, "I guess I should tell you my news. Flick and I are moving in together as soon as we find a bigger place. This isn't the best time to look, so it could take a while, but I wanted you to know in advance. Until then, I'll be staying here once or twice a week. No matter what, I'll give you a month's notice and will pay my share of the rent until we move."

Although Sarah had been expecting that, the news hit hard. "I'm happy for you both, but I'll sure miss you."

"Me, too. Wanna stream a mystery and munch on popcorn?"

It was early yet, and Sarah nodded. The popcorn was yummy and the movie entertaining, yet she glanced often at her phone, hoping to get a message or call from Daniel. She hadn't heard anything from him, but it'd been less than twenty-four hours since he'd left after those kisses. He wasn't working at the firehouse or detailing a car at night, but was probably busy with something. As much as she wanted to talk to him, she resisted reaching out. She wasn't about to chase after the man, plus with her strong feelings and Kendall in his heart, it was best not to contact him.

Still, she wanted to share the news about losing her roomie and finding a replacement, a daunting thought, and whatever else came up.

But her phone remained silent. When the movie ended, she and Erin headed for their respective bedrooms. She put the phone in Do Not Disturb mode and went to bed.

12

Hoping to control his runaway feelings for Sarah, Daniel focused on other things—work at the firehouse, and later in the week, detailing cars, Toad, and anything else that required his attention. He was on his way to Friday night poker when he turned toward her place instead.

Not wanting to show up empty-handed, he stopped at the pet store and picked up something for Puff. Then, at a drug store, he found a package of hair clips she might like. He was almost at her house when he realized she might not be home. Plus, she preferred advance notice. He pulled over and texted. *I'm not far from your place. OK to come over?*

She didn't reply right away, and he figured she was out. Talk about disappointing. His fault for not checking with her sooner. Sitting in the RAV4, he contemplated what to do for the rest of the evening. The poker game didn't appeal to him. Maybe a movie? He was scrolling through options when he heard back. *I'm home and you can come. What time?*

Now?

She replied with a thumbs-up emoji.

When he arrived minutes later, light shining from

her house and at the front door beamed a welcome. Goods in hand, he wiped his feet on the mat and rang the doorbell.

Moments later, she greeted him with a smile every bit as welcoming as the light. "It's good to see you. Come on in."

He couldn't help but return the smile. It'd only been two days, but he felt the same about her. Dressed in jeans, a long-sleeve pullover, and a pair of fuzzy yellow socks, she looked comfortable.

"Smells like popcorn," he said, sniffing appreciatively.

"That's because I just made a batch. I've been knitting up a storm and finished for tonight. I was about to stream a movie. What brings you here?" As he shrugged out of his jacket, she eyed the two small bags he'd set down. "You brought me something again? Keep it up, and you'll spoil me."

"You're easy," he teased, as he reached for her package. "Since you lost one of your hair thingies, I thought you might appreciate a replacement. They aren't tortoiseshell, but maybe you'll like them."

She pulled the two sets of silver clips from the bag. "These are pretty, Daniel. How sweet. Thanks."

She looked so happy. Feeling awkward—he didn't like too much attention—he cleared his throat and pulled out the toy mouse he'd brought for the kitten. "I got this for Puff, something to play with. Where is she, anyway?" And there she was, sashaying over to greet him. "This is for you, little girl."

She sniffed, batted the toy with her paws and hissed when it squeaked. Seconds later, she dragged it to her sleep cage and began to play with it.

"You made her night," Sarah said. "I have soft

drinks or wine to go with the popcorn. What's your preference?"

"I'm a beer man, but wine works, too."

"Wine it is. Do you like mysteries? There's a Sherlock Holmes oldie that looks fun—'Sherlock Holmes and the Secret Weapon' from 1942. Who knows if we'll like it. If we don't, we can always turn it off."

Dog that he was—no offense to Toad—Daniel had other things in mind. Best not to think about that. "I'm game. Where's your roommate?" he wondered, as she pulled out glasses for the wine.

"With her boyfriend. They want to move in together and are looking for a bigger place. That could take a while, but who knows? The rent here is fair but on the steep side for one person. I'll need to find myself a place, too."

"Why not get a new roommate instead? Less hassle that way."

"The idea of rooming with a stranger doesn't appeal to me. But living alone, even if I could afford it... I've never done that and don't think I'd want to. Maybe I *could* live with someone I don't know." She didn't look at all sure about that.

"You have time to figure it out, right? I live by myself. It's not bad."

"Do you get lonely for company?"

"At times. Having a pet helps."

Sarah carried the popcorn bowl, he took the wine, and they headed into the living room. They sat down on the sofa and started the movie. During the scary places, which due to the age of the movie were far and few between, she grabbed hold of Daniel's hand. Before long, his arm was around her and the movie forgotten.

He kissed her, she kissed him back, and things

heated up faster than the other night. He told himself to stop. Then his mind clouded and he forgot everything but the soft woman in his arms.

MAKING out on the sofa with Daniel was wonderful, even better than the kisses at the end of their date the other night. Without quite knowing how she got there, Sarah ended up on his lap, enjoying every moment while her body pressed so close to his. He stroked her back with his big hands, sometimes touching the sides of her breasts, and set her on fire. Like her, he was aroused. She cautioned herself to slow down, but with the passion between them deepening, the warning faded.

Aching for more than kisses, she leaned back a bit and guided his hands to her breasts. He cupped her and let out a low moan. "You're irresistible."

"So are you." Her nipples stood up and begged. As if he somehow knew, he slid his palms under her pullover and toyed with her through her bra. Oh, the pleasure. Wanting more, she shifted restlessly on his lap. She was thinking about taking off some of her clothes when he froze. "We have to stop," he said, and shifted her onto the sofa.

Instantly, she missed his warmth. At the same time, she was relieved that one of them had come to their senses. Shocking and scary how fast her desire had flared. "Thanks for putting the brakes on," she said. "Things are moving way too quickly for me."

"I didn't mean to get carried away, but there's something about you that's hard to resist." He glanced down at his swollen zipper. "Emphasis on *hard*."

Her lips twitched. "Believe me, I noticed. Being

alone together is dangerous. I think we should pull way back and take time apart from each other for a while." She'd planned to do exactly that the last time they'd kissed, but tonight even saying the words made her sad. Startling how quickly she'd gotten used to his company and wanted him in her life. Pretty risky for her.

"I agree and should go." He stood. "I'll let myself out. Take care, Sarah, and have a great weekend."

"You, too, and thanks for the toy and the barrettes."

Way too stirred up to sleep, she channel-surfed and looked for something to distract her from the craving for Daniel. Despite knowing the danger involved, she wanted him. Which she'd realized before, but her crush had grown stronger, to the point of hovering on the edge of love. It was amazing he hadn't picked up on the depth of her feelings for him.

Mad at herself for getting carried away, she reached for her yarn and spent a good hour knitting up a storm—even though she was tired of doing it. She gave herself props for accomplishing so much today. Added to the pieces she'd finished earlier, she had almost enough to last through the craft fair. Fingers crossed.

Drowsy at last, she fell into bed, then realized she needed to keep busy this weekend doing things that took her mind off Daniel. More knitting and getting together with friends would help. Before closing her eyes, she texted Cherry and Mary Jo about having lunch or coffee the following morning or Sunday, but they both had plans with their spouses.

So much for that idea. Erin was with Flick all weekend. Well, shoot. May as well get together with

Lee. She picked up the phone. "Hi, Mom. Am I calling too late?"

"Not at all," her mother said, sounding pleased to hear from her. "Funny, I was about to phone you."

"You were?"

"Mason and I want you to come over tomorrow morning for brunch."

Plans! Sarah brightened up. "I'd like that. What should I bring?"

"Just yourself. Elton is coming, too."

Interesting and curious. "What's up, Mom?"

"I'll tell you tomorrow."

What could she possibly have to say, and why in person? Sarah doubted it was bad news. Lee had sounded more excited than upset. Still, not knowing was both worrisome and irritating. On the positive side, her thoughts now focused on what her mother planned to say instead of her growing passion for Daniel. "I'll find out tomorrow," she told herself, and turned out the light.

13

S aturday morning was cold and gray, fitting Daniel's mood. Once again, fooling around with Sarah the previous evening had created havoc in both his body and his brain and messed with a much-needed good night's sleep. Playing poker would've been a better way to spend Friday night. Ah, well, the hard run he'd scheduled with Tony and Rob should clear his head.

When he arrived at Guff's Lake Resort and Park, Rob was waiting for him at the trailhead where they'd agreed to meet. No sign of Tony yet.

"Sure is cold," Rob said, blowing on his hands before digging into his pockets for gloves.

Daniel agreed, zipping the lightweight jacket he used when running and also donning gloves. While they waited for Tony, his bud squinted at him. "You look like hell. Something go wrong at last night's poker game?"

Not wanting to get into the reason for his bad mood, Daniel shook his head. "I didn't get much sleep. Where's Tony?"

"Right here," the dude said, striding toward them

and frowning at Daniel. "You don't look so good. Getting sick?"

"Quit mothering me, both of you. What I need is a good run."

They took off at a brisk pace and kept it up. Some two hours later, sweaty and exhausted, Daniel felt much better. The three of them stood around, guzzling water, cooling down, and talking. He needed a shower—they all did—but there was no place to do that at the park.

"Now that you're in a better mood, what happened at the poker game?" Rob said.

Daniel wiped his forehead on the hem of his T-shirt, then rezipped the jacket. "I skipped it and went over to Sarah McCone's instead."

Rob's dropped jaw was almost comedic. "Say what?"

Tony grinned. "You like her."

"Afraid so."

"Afraid of what? It's about time you got back in the saddle," Tony said, and clapped his hand on Daniel's shoulder. He would say so—he and his girlfriend Summer were hot and heavy and she was pregnant. "Sarah's cute and way competent at her job."

For some reason, the comment irked him. "True, but I don't know much about her." He knew quite a bit, though—she was smart, warm-hearted, easy to be around, and hot to make out with. "I like being with her, but don't go getting any ideas about me falling for her," he added, both for them and his own sake.

Rob hooted. "Who said anything about that, and why would we? You just started seeing her. Speaking for myself and the rest of the crew, it's a relief you're finally interested in a woman." He paused and looked thoughtful. "You're scratching the back of your neck like you do when something's off. What's the problem?"

"It's obvious she really likes me." The way she kissed him, the look on her face when she was with him. "I told her I'm not into getting serious, but it still feels like I'm leading her on."

"If you're worried about that, then spell it out to her again."

He probably should—unless he'd misread her. Last night they'd agreed to take time apart and cool off, and talking about feelings ought to be done in person. Better to lay low and let things settle for now. Neither of them had known the other long enough to fall in love, so it was all good.

NOT LONG AFTER Sarah parked her car in front of her mom and Mason's place, her brother Elton pulled up behind her. He was twenty-four, three years younger than she was, and they didn't see much of each other. People said they looked similar—they both had hazel eyes and their mom's mouth. Their hair was different, though, hers blonde and wavy like their mom, his reddish and curly like their birth father. "Hi," she said, smiling.

"Hey ya." He flashed a quick grin, then got solemn. "Any idea what this brunch thing is about?"

"Not a clue. Whatever it is, Lee didn't want to tell us over the phone."

"That's weird." Elton frowned. "Do you think she and Mason are okay?"

"Yes. If things weren't going well between them, she wouldn't have invited us to eat with them."

"Good point. Maybe she's pregnant."

Sarah snorted. "At forty-nine? What gave you that idea?"

"A guy on my soccer team has a mom about the same age, and she's expecting. I guess we'll find out. If she is, maybe she'll be a better mom now than she was with us. I sure am hungry."

They headed up the walk to the front door. Some two years ago, Lee and Mason had sold their condo and bought the house. Mason liked to putter around outside, which was evident in the yard. Fall leaves had been raked up, and mulch had been spread around the bushes to prep them for winter.

"Here goes," Elton muttered, knocking at the door —neither of them felt comfortable enough to simply walk in.

Their mother greeted them with hugs, a nice surprise, and Mason's eyes twinkled. Something positive was definitely up.

Sarah and Elton traded confused looks. What if she *was* pregnant? It didn't take long to find out.

"Let's eat before the casserole gets cold," Lee said, and they sat down. Mimosas had been poured for the four of them. Maybe Lee's was a virgin.

Forget food right now. Sarah eyed her mother. "Are you planning to tell us what's going on or keep us in suspense?"

"I guess now is a good time. We have fun news." Lee glanced at her husband. "Do you want to tell them?"

"You do it, hon."

"It'll be my pleasure. Mason has been promoted to construction manager, and he got a huge raise." She lifted her cocktail up. "Here's to you, love!"

They all took healthy sips. Then, beaming, Lee

leaned in close to her Mason and kissed him soundly on the lips.

Elton made a face. "Cool it with the mushy stuff, will ya?"

Relieved her mom wasn't pregnant, Sarah grinned. "Congratulations."

"We're celebrating with a two-week cruise to the Caribbean."

"The trip you've been saving for," Sarah remembered. "That sounds fun. When are you going?"

"The day after Thanksgiving. Business at the spa is slow then."

Once again, Sarah and her brother exchanged looks. This time, Elton asked the question. "So no Thanksgiving this year?"

"We'll still have it, but I don't want to cook or deal with the leftovers. We're going to eat at the Hearthstone at Guff's Lake Resort."

The same place where Daniel and his family were going? Sarah could hardly believe her ears. "It's probably too late to get a reservation there," she said, hoping that was the case. She didn't want to run into him, which might stir up Lee and Mason's curiosity.

Mason nodded. "I worried about that. When I called last week, they were full up in the evening, but I was able to reserve a table at one o'clock."

"Why didn't you tell us?" Elton said.

"We wanted to surprise you, and we have. Surprise!"

Sarah couldn't summon a semblance of enthusiasm. She wanted to tell Daniel, but they'd agreed to give each other space, and she assumed that included calling each other or texting. He certainly hadn't contacted her. Best hold off and let him know later. She did the next best thing and texted Erin.

14

Crew members at the firehouse prepared dinner on a rotating basis, each one taking a turn. Tuesday was Daniel's night. After lunch, he headed to the kitchen to prep for the meal. Early the previous day, he'd made a large vat of split pea soup and frozen it in the firehouse's big kitchen freezer. Making the salad required little focus, freeing his mind to think about Sarah. It'd been three days since those hot kisses, and he was still stirred up. As agreed, he'd steered clear of contacting her. So had she. Want to or not, he missed her.

Salad finished, he pulled the soup from the freezer, along with several store-bought loaves of garlic bread. Soon after he set both on the counter to thaw and slid the salad into the fridge, a loud beeper sounded. The voice of the woman he couldn't stop thinking about filled the air as she alerted the crew to the emergency—a three-alarmer—the rating for an extremely dangerous fire.

According to the concise information she shared, the fire had started at a building under construction and quickly spread to several attached townhouses where people lived. Firefighters in all nearby areas had been called in to help, as well as those off-duty.

Both engines at the station were deployed, the smaller of the two engineered by Max, with Adam in the second seat as befitted the lieutenant. In the larger engine, Liam drove, with Captain Comings riding shotgun.

Daniel and some of his teammates rode with Liam as he sped toward the address. On the drive, no one said much. Daniel hadn't been involved with a three-alarm fire since he'd lived in Sacramento. Unwanted memories flooded back. The second-degree burns on his shoulder and upper arm, the trip to the hospital, followed by the accident that'd taken Kendall's life, and the grief that was still with him. Bile flooded his mouth. He couldn't afford to think about that now. He swallowed it back.

They made it to the site in record time, quickly donned their SCBSs—self-contained breathing apparatuses—and jumped into action along with a large number of other firefighters joining them. Getting control of the fire wasn't easy, and for hours everyone fought valiantly. When at last it ended, the building under construction was declared a total loss. The fire that spread to the townhouses had burned so hot that several windows melted, and two of the floors collapsed.

Owen and Rafe suffered second-degree burns, and Nate sprained his ankle. Many who lived in the ruined duplexes had been at work and missed the horrendous event and likely lost everything. Same with the inhabitants at home in their units who'd quickly evacuated, many with nothing but their lives and the clothes on their backs.

Miraculously, no one died—as yet. In all, fifteen people ended up in the hospital, four in critical condition. Two dogs and a cat were taken to a veterinary hospital to receive treatment.

"I'm proud of all of you," Captain Comings said on the silent ride back to the firehouse. "And I pray the four patients in critical condition survive and thrive."

Daniel fervently agreed as did everyone else. "If ever the benefit fund is needed, this is it," he said. "I sure hope people have insurance." In case the fund wasn't enough.

Back at the station, exhausted men showered and changed into clean clothes. Over dinner, they shoveled in the soup and garlic bread and spoke quietly among themselves about the afternoon. A fire like that didn't happen often, and this one had been a doozy.

Later, as beat as Daniel was, he was too antsy to sleep. Forget not contacting Sarah. Tonight, seeing her was as vital to him as breathing. He reached for his cell phone.

Within seconds, she picked up. "I'm so glad you called. What a horrific day. Are you okay?"

Not as bad as he'd been before she answered. Having no idea why reaching her was so important, he paused. "I've been better. I know we decided to give each other space, but I need to see you." Needed her, period. "Will you come to the firehouse? I'll meet you in the visitor's area." Aka the lobby. "Let Betsy at the front desk, know when you arrive."

"I'll be there in under ten minutes."

~

Daniel entered the lobby to wait for Sarah. Betsy, who took over as receptionist when Miranda's shift ended, greeted him with surprise. "I thought sure you'd be upstairs."

"Can't sleep. I'm going to take a walk with Sarah McCone."

She gave an understanding nod. "After a day like yours, it's good to have someone to talk to. Everyone appreciates Sarah's level head and calm voice during emergencies. I rarely get to see her. It'll be nice to say hello."

Stifling the urge to pace, he stared blankly at the station's first fire truck, circa 1913, displayed in the center of the room. He didn't have to wait long before Sarah blew through the door, bringing a gust of cold night air with her. She wore a yellow wool hat, no doubt made by her own hand, and a parka. The mere sight of her was like a balm to his sorry soul. "Hey," he said, managing a faint smile for the first time in hours. "Let's go for a walk and find a café around here."

"Sounds good to me. Hi, Betsy," she greeted the receptionist. "It's good to see you."

"You too, Sarah. Enjoy your walk."

Daniel nodded at the woman. "Call if you need me," he said, crossing his fingers she wouldn't.

As soon as they exited the firehouse, he started to reach for Sarah, then hesitated. "Is it okay to hold your hand?"

"That's fine, if you don't mind that it's ice cold."

"No gloves tonight?"

"I was in such a rush to get here I left them at home. Talk to me."

Exactly what he needed to hear. He clasped her hand and yep, it was cold. "This has been a terrible day."

"I know," she said, and squeezed his fingers. "Is everyone okay?"

He told her about Owen, Rafe, and Nate. "They'll be fine. The hospital discharged them in time for dinner."

"That's great news. What about the people in the townhouse?"

He shared the details he knew about. "Four are in critical care, two of them battling for their lives," he finished, his voice breaking with the agony he felt. For the man and for a past he couldn't change.

"The best hospital around for trauma patients—they're in good hands," she soothed. "You look like you need a hug." Right there on the sidewalk and without waiting for any reaction from him, she wrapped her arms around his middle.

God above, he needed this. He felt her warmth despite the heavy coats they both wore. The urge to bare his soul gripped him. "There's a small café nearby that's open till late. Let's go there."

The place was all but deserted. They sat down at a table and ordered decaf coffee.

"How's the knitting going?" he asked, desperate to talk about normal things and forget about the disastrous afternoon.

"Nicely." She filled him in on that, reminded him that Puff was getting spayed the following morning, and other things that had nothing to do with the fire. "Over the weekend, my mom and Mason invited me and my brother to brunch. Apparently Mason got a promotion and will earn a much bigger paycheck. You'll never guess what they decided."

"No, but I expect I'm about to find out," he replied and cocked his eyebrows.

"They're celebrating with a cruise. It starts the day after Thanksgiving. She doesn't want to cook or deal with dishes and leftovers, so she and Mason made reservations at the Hearthstone for Thanksgiving dinner in the same time slot as your family." She rolled her eyes. "Can you believe that?"

He sat back. "Seriously?"

"I'm afraid so. If my mother sees you, there's no telling what she might do or say. After you taught the class at the spa, she hinted that we're perfect for each other."

News to him. "No way. She wouldn't try to stir things up during the Thanksgiving feast, would she?"

"Knowing Lee, she might. She's never been very involved in Elton's life or mine, but in the last few years she's become very interested in seeing us settled down."

"Don't forget my folks riding me to 'get out there' and meet someone. Things could get weird."

"Can you imagine your parents and mine pushing us to be together?"

Her sigh of misery tickled a smile out of him.

"It's not funny, so what's with the grin? Not that I mind. It's good to see you more cheerful."

He wasn't all that happy, but feeling better by the minute. "Don't blow what might happen out of proportion. Even if they do strongly hint that we should get together, it wouldn't be that bad. My family won't be around for more than a few days, and yours will be leaving town for a cruise."

He yawned, and her eyes twinkled. "I think you're ready for bed, Mr. O'Dwyer."

"I can hardly believe this, but I am. You started your day hours before I started mine. You must be tired, too. I really appreciate your coming here. Thanks for taking my mind off today for a while." It meant a lot to him. He felt closer to her than ever, and was grateful she was in his life.

"No thanks necessary. Special circumstances made tonight a necessity, something friends do for each other."

He liked that. Friends didn't have sex so they'd be safe, he assured himself, ignoring the possibility that some did. So why was he thinking about that now, when it should've been the furthest thought from his mind? Because, horndog that he was, the woman who kept messing with his head and fanning his desires was right there, front and center.

They headed toward the firehouse and the lot where she'd parked. He wanted to kiss her, but planted a chaste peck on her cheek instead. "Thanks for tonight."

"I'm honored you wanted to be with me. Now it's my turn for a favor."

"Name it."

"First thing tomorrow, I drop Puff off, and even though I know female cats get spayed all the time and it's pretty much a quick and easy operation, I'm going to need a distraction to keep me from worrying. If you don't have any appointments in the morning, would you mind if I came over? It's my turn, plus I'd like to see where you live."

He was on the fence about that, wanting her despite the danger being alone together posed. But she'd asked and it was fair play to do his part when she needed him. "Okay, but I have an appointment with a Cadillac at eleven."

"No problem—I'll come early. Okay?" Her eyes grew big and pleading, almost as if she sensed the battle inside him. "I'll even bring breakfast."

He opened his mouth to suggest they meet somewhere instead, a safer idea, but she wasn't finished.

"I realize we made a decision not to see each other

for a while, and I promise not to stay long, just enough to keep my mind off Puff while she's under the knife. All I need is your address."

No hetero male could resist those eyes or the slightly pursed lips. Despite his grave concerns about the whole thing, he gave in. "See you then."

15

The following morning, Sarah pressed the doorbell at Daniel's three-story apartment building door shortly before nine o'clock. He buzzed her in right away, as if he'd been waiting for her. He lived on the second floor and his door was open. He met her there. Dressed in black jeans and a gray, long-sleeve Henley shirt with the top three buttons unfastened, he was definitely swoon-worthy. Oh, those shoulders...She wanted to melt but hadn't come over to make an idiot of herself. Instead of smiling, he seemed subdued, and she wondered if coming over had been a bad idea.

He glanced at the hefty breakfast sack in her hands and reached for it. "I'll take that and—"

Toad dashed—make that hopped—toward her, his furry tail wagging. "I'm excited to see you, too, boy," she greeted, and handed the breakfast stuff to Daniel. "You mentioned that he hopped when he was excited, but I had no idea till now how adorable he looks when he does it."

"Did you hear that, fella? I'm not sure about the adorable part, but you are pretty cute."

Tail wagging, he sniffed her. "You smell breakfast,

huh? I'm sorry I didn't bring you any treats. I hate to break it to you, but this is for us humans, and I'm pretty sure yours is about to eat all his. Are you hungry, Daniel?"

"Sure am. Whatever you picked up from Rosemary's is making my mouth water. The fresh coffee's this way." He gestured ahead of them and led her through a short hallway and into the compact kitchen. His little apartment was about half the square footage of her cottage, just right for a man living alone. They took turns washing their hands at the kitchen sink.

While Daniel filled the mugs with coffee, she found plates and utensils and brought out the breakfast containers along with two muffins. As they sat down, she noted the framed photo on the wall across the room of him with a beautiful woman, their arms around each other and smiles on their faces. It wasn't difficult to guess her identity: Kendall, the woman he still loved and cherished.

Stifling a wince at the reminder she was all too aware of, Sarah considered mentioning how happy the couple looked, but this seemed the wrong time. Besides, right now she preferred to focus on other things. "I hope you don't mind the same meal you ordered when we had breakfast there," she said.

"Are you kidding? That breakfast special is a favorite of mine. Let me at it."

They'd barely dug in when Toad wandered over and sat on the floor beside her. He sniffed her jeans and the busy tail wagged again. "I won't be dropping any food on the floor today," she said.

"Good, because I don't feed him that way and don't want to start. How are you feeling about Puff this morning?"

"Much better now that Dr. Gruen has her."

"Did she seem upset?"

"A little uneasy. She was clingy and, of course, hungry. I think she sensed I was nervous, but I'm not anymore. It's a routine procedure, she's in good hands, and I'm here with you. Thanks for letting me come over."

"Like you said last night, it's what friends do."

He was such a great guy. "Erin offered to bring her home after work tonight. I doubt she'll stay at the house long, though. She's been sleeping at Flick's a lot. Puff will have to wear that special onesie thing I told you about. I'm not looking forward to that or what will probably be an unhappy night for her, but I'm sure we'll both survive.

"Gwen offered to stop by and check on her tomorrow, and I'm so glad she did. I think she may be strapped for cash, and of course, I'm going to pay her. If she likes helping out with cats and decides to do more of it, I'll recommend her to friends and suggest she post a sign on the bulletin board at the Animal Care Clinic." Realizing she was rambling, Sarah stifled herself and sipped coffee.

"Good idea. Sounds like everything's taken care of with Puff, and you don't have to worry anymore."

"Yes, and a big relief." The dog continued to sniff her pant legs and even whined a bit. "You know I'm not going to feed you," she reminded him, and glanced at Daniel. "I wonder what he's sniffing about?"

"You always smell good."

"Do I?" Must be the shampoo she used, as she didn't wear fragrance. She thought a minute. "Do you think he smells Puff? Earlier this morning, she climbed up my jeans a few times."

"Who knows, he might. He's met her more than

once. I think he likes her—as much as any dog who knows a cat."

"I'm guessing she feels that way about him, too." Like Daniel and me, Sarah thought. "Maybe they can get together sometime for a play date, if that's possible between a dog and a kitten. Wouldn't that be something? If it worked, which it might or might not." As soon as the words were out, she wanted to call them back. She and Daniel needed their space and weren't likely to get together again. Too bad she enjoyed being with him so much.

During breakfast, they were both quiet and focused on the food. At least she was. For a man who had a big appetite, he wasn't exactly eating with gusto, and he looked exhausted. "You didn't sleep well last night and you're not hungry, either," she pointed out. "You're still dealing with what happened yesterday, which is understandable."

"True that." He set his fork down and scrubbed a hand over his face. "It'll take a while to get past what happened. Heck, I doubt I ever will."

"I'm sure your teammates are going through the same thing. That fire was the worst. You could always see one of the therapists in the area who focus on fire trauma."

Toad went to the back door and wagged his tail to go out, and Daniel let him into the fenced yard. Then he returned to the table and went on without a word about therapy. "The thing is, it brought up a lot of stuff I don't think about anymore." The agonized expression darkening his face screamed that he was in emotional turmoil.

Poor guy. Wondering if he'd open up but not about to press him for details, she picked at the remnants on her plate and left him to his private thoughts.

Her silence paid off. A moment later, he pushed his plate away. "Do you remember the day we rescued Puff, and I told you about Kendall?" He nodded toward the photo.

"Of course." She'd been both shocked and dismayed. "I noticed that photograph as soon as we came into the kitchen. What a beautiful woman." In a class Sarah couldn't begin to compete with. But then, she'd known that long ago.

"She was." He glanced away from both her and the photo. After clearing his throat, he went on. "I left some things out about the accident that took her life. The day she died started out like any other. We had breakfast together, then she left for work. She loved growing things and had a job at a nursery. Back then, Toad was still a pup. I dropped him off at doggie daycare and headed for the firehouse in Sacramento."

Even without knowing the full story, the combination of his tormented expression and the pain in his voice made her ache for him. "You don't have to talk about this unless you want to."

"It's time I told someone the full story, and I'd rather it be you than some therapist." He swallowed. "Not long after I arrived at the firehouse that day, we got an alert calling us to a brutal, three-alarm monster similar to the one here in town yesterday."

He didn't look at her, instead stared into space as if lost in the memory of it. "We battled that demon for what seemed forever before we contained and then destroyed it. Several of us were injured. I had second-degree burns similar to what Owen and Rafe suffered yesterday. I also sprained my ankle like Nate. I was in the hospital for a couple of hours, then advised to go home and rest. One of the guys from the station who wasn't injured offered to drive me and a few more of us home, but Kendall insisted on picking me up. If I'd told her not to..." He sucked in a shuddering breath, then blew it out. "She'd be alive today."

Opening up that way meant he trusted her, and Sarah realized they'd reached another milestone in their relationship. Her heart swelled with dangerous feelings she didn't even try to deny. She sensed he didn't want her to comment and knew he wasn't comfortable with a show of sympathy. Which didn't mean he couldn't use a comforting hug similar to what she'd given him the night before. Somber and silent, she stood up, moved to his side, and opened her arms. He looked up at her with such misery her own eyes teared up. As soon as he rose, she wrapped her arms around him. He sighed and hugged her back. "How did you know I needed this every bit as much as I did last night? Come on." His firm arms left her and he grasped her hand.

"Where are we going?" she asked, puzzled.

"I think you agree that due to our height differences, hugging each other while standing is awkward. I need to sit down and want to talk more, and the couch is in the living room."

It wasn't a big space by any means, and the large piece of furniture angled between two corners facing a large flat TV all but filled the room. He sat down and pulled her beside him. The masculine, brown leather couch was surprisingly soft and comfortable. He wrapped his arms around her again. No words uttered, no kisses or caresses, simply being together. Showing her his vulnerabilities meant a great deal to her, and she wanted the moment to last as long as possible.

There was nothing sexual about any of it, and this was not the time to get turned on. It happened anyway. Her heart expanded and certain body parts tingled for attention. The heat she felt scared her, but oh, how she wanted him.

Almost as if he sensed her internal struggle, he nuzzled her neck. Forget tingling. The sensitive parts inside her went full sizzle. Afraid of her feelings, she pulled away. "What's happening here, Daniel? We agreed not to get physical."

"I'm well aware of that, but I'm fighting a losing battle with myself. I don't want to let you go, I want to lose myself in you. It's a bad idea. I know that, but—"

No, it isn't! her body argued, although she acknowledged he was right. Yet, as he released her, every inch of her body protested. "I want the same thing," she admitted, "but I don't think sex is the best way to forget your troubles, at least not for long."

"Hadn't thought about that. You're not easy to resist when you look at me like you haven't eaten in days and I'm food."

Unable to lie, she told the truth. "I can't help how I feel. It's been a long time since I've been with a man, and I—" her cell phone rang. "It's the Animal Care Clinic." Grateful for the interruption that'd saved her from confessing that she wanted him now regardless what she'd said moments ago, she turned away from his gaze. The news was good, and she pivoted toward him. "Puff did well. Erin's bringing her home later this afternoon."

"That's great. You were about to say something when the phone call interrupted."

Share that she wanted to make love more than anything? She didn't dare. "I was going to say it's nice being held."

"Better than nice. How about a hug for your good news about Puff."

Unable to resist, she scooted closer to him, dangerous as it was. Desire overpowering her need to be cautious, she raised up and kissed him. For a moment, he went still. Then, with a growl, he made love to her mouth with kisses every bit as passionate as the last time. Before long, they were lying on the sofa, his hands under her blouse and his fingers inside her bra. Wild with hunger, she moaned and raised her hips in a silent plea to turn his attention farther south.

He left her aching breasts alone, unzipped her jeans, and slid his fingers into her panties. There wasn't much room to navigate, but he managed to touch her *there*. She climaxed right away. When it was over, he grinned.

"That happened embarrassingly fast," she said.

"Trust me, it was hot."

"For me, but not you." She pulled herself together and scooted away from him. "As much as I want sex with you, I'm relieved we stopped. Despite the way I acted, I'm not ready."

"I understand, but I'm not sorry for what happened. I don't think you are, either." He tucked her hair behind his ears, sending the crazy feelings through her again. His watch beeped and he glanced at it. "It's time for me to go detail that Caddy."

Had she stayed at his house that long? She checked her own watch and discovered she had. She wasn't pleased with losing herself like that, but at least she'd pulled herself together before she did something she'd regret.

While she retrieved her coat, Daniel let Toad back in. The dog woofed softly at her. "Goodbye to you, too," she told him.

"If we want to stay out of trouble, we can't do this again," he said on the way to the door.

"Right—we need to give each other space, like we agreed before." Even as she spoke the words, she longed for that kind of trouble. "Bye, Daniel."

She hurried out the door.

AT HOME again after leaving Daniel, Sarah pulled out her knitting supplies and warned herself not to think about him, for all the good that did. As she knitted up a storm, memories of the deliciousness from this morning crowded her mind. His mouth, his skilled hands...she was still floating in sensation. Had she ever been this turned on?

"No more of that," she warned out loud. She didn't want to get hurt, but couldn't stop thinking about him and itching for more.

Midafternoon, tired of her inability to put him out of her mind, she left the house. At the pet shop where she'd been so many times lately, they knew her by name, she bought Puff treats for when Erin brought her home. Then she stopped at a store and picked up nibblies for herself. She returned to the little house shortly before Erin arrived.

The kitten looked sleepy. "Hello, sweet Puff," she murmured. "How are you feeling?"

Of course, her pet didn't answer, but Erin did. "She's still a bit drowsy, but she did eat something earlier. Dr. Gruen gave her an injection to control the pain that lasts about three days. If you have questions or concerns, call us, and bring her in if you need to."

"I will." Sarah set Puff gently in her sleeping cage. Immediately, she went to sleep.

"We haven't talked about Thanksgiving," Erin said.

"I can't believe both your family and Daniel's are going to the Hearthstone."

"Neither can we. We need to talk about that, and soon. What are you doing over the holiday?"

"My parents won't be in town, and Flick's family are going to their cabin in the mountains. It's not a big place, so we decided to make other plans. We're taking a long weekend. We booked reservations in Tucson. It'll be nice and warm there."

"Lucky you. Sounds fun."

"It will be. Anything new with Daniel?"

Eager to confide in her friend, Sarah told her about the three-alarm fire the previous day and how shaken Daniel had been. She didn't mention what had happened to Kendall or any of that—it wasn't her story to tell. Most everyone knew she'd passed away, but not the rest. That said, Sarah had no problems spilling the details about that morning. "I was nervous about Puff, so I went to Daniel's for breakfast." Her face warmed.

Naturally, Erin noticed. "Out with it. What happened?"

Too much and not nearly enough. "Let's just say we did quite a bit of kissing and other things."

"I like what I'm hearing. And?"

"No, we didn't have sex, even though we wanted to. He's interested in me both sexually and as a friend, and you know how crazy I am about him. I don't want him to find out."

Erin gave a sage nod. "You're worried that sharing your feelings will scare him off."

"I guarantee it would. He doesn't want anything serious and doesn't think I do, either."

"That's exactly what Flick and I talked about on

our second date. Back then, I hadn't fallen for him yet." Erin let out a soft sigh. "And look at us now."

"Rub it in, why don't you. As much as I want sex with Daniel, I'm not ready and he knows it. How many times have I sworn not to rush into anything? Well, this morning I came close to doing exactly that. I don't want to get hurt."

"It's a risk, for sure." Erin paused. "You didn't ask, but as your bestie I have to share my thoughts."

"Please do."

"You're already totally gone over him. That's a done deal that having sex won't change. And FYI, you're not jumping in. You've been wild about him for a while."

"Remember, it started as a crush." A huge one. "I didn't get to know him better until recently." Erin glanced at the ceiling, and Sarah eyed her. "You think I should go ahead and indulge?"

"Only if you're ready. Maybe you stay together, maybe you don't—we're not seers and can't know the future. No matter what happens, if you part ways, it's gonna hurt. In the meantime, the man has sexual needs and so do you. You may as well enjoy being with him in every way for as long as it lasts."

Sarah thought of something else and frowned. "I don't want him thinking I'm desperate."

"Why would he? If you're worried about it, prove you aren't."

"Exactly how would I do that?"

"Stay busy, don't nag him, and don't let him talk you into sex until you decide you're ready."

"I'm doing all those things now."

"Then you get a gold star."

16

The day after the hottest fooling around of his life, Daniel phoned Sarah when her shift ended. To get an update on Puff, discuss Thanksgiving, and simply because he enjoyed talking to her. Also to gauge her feelings on anything else on her mind, namely yesterday morning.

"How's Puff doing?" he asked after the usual greetings.

"Still groggy from the medications Dr. Gruen gave her, but according to him, that should wear off in the next day or two. How are you?"

Like his crewmates, still angsting over the fire. "Hanging in there. Your company and being with you both Tuesday evening and yesterday morning helped a lot. Thanks for listening." He lowered his voice. "And for the rest."

She went silent and he wondered if she was grateful they hadn't had sex and having second thoughts about their insanely sizzling morning together, or if like him, she thought about it all the time. He needed to find out. "Are you okay about yesterday?"

"I think you know the answer to that—we talked about it before I left. How was your day?"

Filled with steamy fantasies of pleasuring her, but he wasn't going there. "Not bad. I went for a run with Toad. Dang, it was cold. I detailed three cars—two clients of mine and one of Rob's. Lately, he's been busy with other things. It's a good thing I'm available to fill in for him."

"We're all busy with one thing or another. I want you to know that I appreciate your concern for Puff."

"I've been thinking about both you and her since you left my place. Your company was much appreciated when I really needed you, and the breakfast was tasty. I polished it off at lunch."

"Good to know. We help each other. It's what friends do, right?"

Friends, he reminded himself. Red-hot friends. He heard her yawn. "Late night?"

"Puff didn't sleep well. I hope she's better tonight. She woke me up several times, and you know how early I leave for work."

"I won't keep you much longer. We should talk about Thanksgiving."

"It's almost here."

"A week from today, coming up way too soon for me. My family arrives sometime Tuesday afternoon. They want a tour of the firehouse that evening, if possible. Wednesday, we'll have breakfast at Rosemary's. Then I'll show them around Guff's Lake Park."

"A full day, sure to be fun. I'll bet you're looking forward to seeing everyone."

Despite some apprehension about the visit, he was. "It'll be good to see them. Maybe they'll lay off the comments about my single status. At least my sister and her husband leave me alone about it." A much-appreciated change from when they'd gone silent along with the parents after Kendall's death.

"We're in the same boat, but it's a holiday and they'll behave. If they don't, we'll survive."

"There's that voice of common sense I admire every time you guide us firefighters through emergencies. Seeing each other at the Hearthstone could be a problem. I don't want them getting any ideas."

"Why would they, when we haven't said anything? Anyway, the place will be packed and we may not run into each other. Although we do have reservations in the same time slot, so it could happen. It shouldn't be a big deal—we'll say hello and that will be that. Lee hasn't mentioned you since you did the safety preparedness class at the spa, and I don't expect that to change. After all, she has no idea I was seeing you. And now, we're not seeing each other anymore."

"The space thing—right," he acknowledged, but he'd figured that meant taking a short break apart. She made it sound permanent, and that didn't sit well at all. "How long before we can start seeing each other again? I gotta be honest here, I still want to be with you."

"Me, too, Daniel, but when we're together, things tend to get out of hand."

"Don't I know it." The mere thought of touching her sweet body turned him on. For the dozenth time today, he started to get aroused, and willed his body to behave. "Surely you know how much I enjoy your company. We have a lot in common—we can talk to each other about all kinds of stuff, and neither of us is interested in getting serious. If you don't want to have sex, we won't," he added, though it killed him to say so. "But let's not make this space thing permanent."

She made a sound that reminded him of the moan

of pleasure she'd let out just before she'd climaxed. "Don't, Daniel."

Unsure what she was referring to, he frowned. "Don't what?"

"Just—never mind. I can't talk about sex right now. I have to get up early. Goodnight."

Sweet dreams," he said, all hot and bothered.

And wondered how he'd ever fall asleep.

SARAH SET the phone aside and blew out a breath. Everything Daniel said made her ache for him, including the longing in his voice which echoed her own. Was that so terrible? "Don't jump into anything," she counseled herself, while Erin's advice that she already loved him and may as well enjoy him while he was interested hummed through her mind. She was so confused. What was the rush, anyway?

There was no need to decide right this minute. Yet over the next few days, despite her own advice to move slowly, she fantasized endlessly about making love with him. It made her cranky. If that wasn't bad enough, he was giving her the space she'd suggested and wanted. No calls or texts. This also made her cranky.

What was wrong with her? She couldn't have it both ways. Thank goodness for knitting and Puff, who was sleeping better and seemed to have rallied. Poor little girl hated wearing the onesie that kept her away from her sutures but was growing more like her usual perky self by the day.

By Saturday afternoon, she'd knitted a ton of scarves and hats and a bunch of cute ornaments. During rest breaks, she'd begun packing the finished products in labeled cartons for the craft fair, which began the day after Thanksgiving.

The hats and mittens she'd made for the family she'd adopted had been wrapped in holiday paper and set aside. She'd also started a sweater for Elton and a cozy afghan for her mom and Mason. Those went in the unfinished projects box to finish before Christmas. By then, she was stir-crazy and sick of her own company. Ready to pick up dinner and treat herself to a movie, she blew Puff a kiss. "I'll be back soon, okay?"

She donned her coat and opened the door, closed it, and was about to lock up when she realized she'd forgotten her purse. All that knitting had made her an airhead. As she turned to grab it, Daniel pulled into her driveway. Wondering what he wanted and way too anxious to find out, she shut the door behind her again and watched him exit the RAV4. In a leather jacket and fleece cap, he looked delicious. Her heart beat furiously with love and desire, which she did her best to curb as he parked and headed toward her. "What are you doing here?" she asked, her silent internal battle making her sound less than welcoming even to her own ears.

Frowning, he stopped a few feet away. "You're ticked that I'm not giving you space and that I showed up unannounced."

"Partly." Mostly at her physical reaction, which she couldn't seem to control. "I've been knitting nonstop since early this morning and almost have enough for the holiday fair. I should probably keep working, but if I touch one more knitting needle today, I swear I'll go mad. I was about to get myself something to eat, then come back, sip wine, and veg out. What brings you over?"

"Thought I'd stop by and see how you and Puff are doing."

"We're okay, but I'm suffering here. I keep thinking about that phone call the other night—everything you said was a plea for us to have sex." How was she supposed to fight what she so badly yearned for?

"I also said if you don't want to, we won't."

"You definitely uttered those words, but with your voice all low and seductive...Darn you for making me burn for you!"

"Do I?" He flashed a smile that quickly faded. "I can't help how I feel, but I meant what I said. There's a name for what we're both experiencing—a situationship."

"What's that?"

"A TikTok term for a sexual relationship that's more than a casual hookup. Intimacy and dating are involved with no expectations of a formal commitment. Fits us to a tee, right? But keep in mind what I said the other night on the phone—whether or not we have sex is up to you. And that's okay. What I can't handle is the thought of not seeing you anymore. Admit it—you don't want that, either."

True, but the 'situationship' idea didn't sit well with her. On the other hand, it was a way to have the sex she so craved with him. She sighed and thought about how to explain herself without confessing she loved him. "We want different things."

"Not true. I want to be with you, Sarah, and you want to be with me." An icy wind gusted, and she shivered. He did, too. "Why don't we go inside and talk more about this."

She didn't see the point of that. "I prefer to stay out here. We shouldn't be alone together," she reminded him and herself. Thanks to the wind, her hair had come loose again. She shoved it back—for all the good that did.

"Then we'll have dinner somewhere around other people and talk there." After another gust, he frowned and moved closer. "There goes your hair again." He tucked it behind her ear and brushed her cheek with his cold fingers. She shivered, this time not from the cold. The man was impossible to resist. "I'm hungry," she grumbled.

"You sound hangry to me. I'm getting there myself. You were about to go out, so pick a place and we'll eat together."

She gave in and nodded.

"Great. What do you feel like eating?"

Who cared about food? She wanted him. Not tonight, though, she hastily assured herself, although with Erin's suggestion to go ahead and indulge playing through her mind, she was strongly tempted. *Not yet*, she silently ordered herself. "Burgers and something chocolatey for dessert sound good."

"How about The Rogue? Their hot fudge sundaes are good, and there's plenty of room inside. Even if it is a Saturday night, we should be able to get a table."

Her mouth started to water. "I'll follow you in my car so you don't have to come all the way back here."

"Don't be silly. One car is enough. Traffic shouldn't be too bad. Let's go. By the way, I have to be home by ten to let Toad out before he settles in for the night."

"Surely dinner won't take that long. Let me grab my purse."

Inside, she quickly tidied up the living room, then decanted a bottle of red wine. "Don't get the wrong idea," she told Puff, who was watching her every move. "I'll come straight back after dinner, and I'm going to behave myself."

The kitten meowed as if to say, "No, you won't. You want him and you have to have him."

"That doesn't mean I plan to do anything about it tonight—there's no rush." Puff shook her head, and she guessed the cat knew better. "You're too smart for your own good. See you later."

17

Determined to convince Sarah not to cut their relationship off and also have a good time that evening, Daniel headed for The Rogue. She was important to him, and he intended to assure her that he was okay with hanging out, period, no matter how much he wanted her. She was the first—the only—woman who'd interested him since Kendall's death. Losing her wasn't an option. There his thoughts ended.

On the drive, which due to light traffic didn't take long, they talked about the music playing on the radio and debated whether it would snow soon—benign subjects that didn't stir up the heavier stuff. The real conversation would wait till they'd put something in their bellies.

The smells of good food in The Rogue ratcheted up his hunger and made him salivate. As expected, the place was crowded, but not packed. A couple at a nearby table was about to leave. "See those people paying their bill? Let's grab their seats," he said, leaning in close so Sarah could hear over the noise. The light scent he couldn't identify but associated with her flirted dangerously with the desire he meant to tamp down. The way she trembled when his lips almost grazed her ear didn't help. He barely resisted stealing a kiss.

"You found seats for us," she commented, avoiding his eyes and focusing on the couple about to leave.

In no time, a server cleared and cleaned the table, then took their orders. It wasn't until they wolfed down the meal and enjoyed their dessert that he realized the noise level in the room was too high for the conversation he wanted to have. "It's way too loud in here for us to talk," he said.

"You're right," she agreed, almost cheerful. "I guess that means we can skip it."

"Uh-uh, you can't wiggle out of this that easily. We'll continue this at your place."

"Can't we do it on the way there instead?"

"Nope. I won't be able to focus on our discussion while I drive."

"You're serious about this," she grumbled, and he wasn't sure whether it was because she didn't want to talk or they'd be alone in her house.

"No fooling around, I promise. We'll have a conversation, then if you want to kick me out, I'll leave."

She barely said a word on the drive. Still in a bad mood, he figured, even with her stomach full. Time to pull back and regroup. "It's obvious from your silence that you don't want to talk. I can't force you, so I'll drop you at your place and go on my way."

"I'm quiet because I've been thinking a lot about things. I changed my mind about us talking—we definitely should," she said, surprising him.

Could be she liked the idea of them continuing to see each other. Either that, or she'd decided she really wanted to end contact. Total bummer, and he decided to opt for the former. A guy could hope. "Great." He parked in her driveway and they headed for the front door. Inside, he hung his jacket on the door knob.

Puff scampered toward him. "Hey, there. You seem pretty spunky," he said, looking forward to the upcoming conversation.

"She's improving by the day."

"That's good news. Can I pick her up?"

"As long as you're careful. She's still healing."

"So I see by the bodysuit." He knelt down, and laid his hand, palm up, on the carpet. "Climb on if you're in the mood." Giving a short meow, she did just that. Chuckling, he carefully rose from the ground. As soon as she was against his chest, she began to purr. "Missed me, huh?"

Sarah, was wide-eyed, either with shock or something else. "Was I not supposed to pick her up?" he asked, and started to set her back on the rug.

"Feel free to hold her. She doesn't see you often, but obviously still adores you. I didn't think cats imprinted on humans they didn't live with, but she's certainly bonded with you. When she's ready to get down, then yeah, put her down." She pivoted toward an open bottle of wine. "I opened this before you picked me up. I know you prefer beer, but this is what I have. Do you want a glass?"

"Sure." He couldn't help but think about what he really wanted—her. Forget that. Having her in his life was what mattered most. Suddenly, Puff meowed like she'd had enough. Careful not to hurt her, he placed her on the rug.

"Why don't we sip our drinks at the table," Sarah said after she poured the wine.

The time had come to have that talk, but he wanted to know more about her change of heart. Instead of leading the conversation, he let her start. "You say you've been thinking?"

"You first."

If she preferred that, okay. He'd already spelled things out without making the impact he'd hoped for. At a loss what to say, he ran his finger around the rim of his glass, then ran with a fresh way to say it. "I'll be straight with you. In the short time we've gotten to know each other—" He broke off to clear his throat. "You mean a lot to me, and I don't want to lose you. As much as I want you physically, spending time with you is most important to me."

"I understood the first time you said it, and it's just as sweet to hear now," she said, and gestured at the wine bottle. "How about a refill?" He shook his head and she left the bottle on the table. "If you're finished—"

He wasn't. "Not quite," he said. She nodded and he continued. "This relationship happened fast, but our close friendship is real. I can talk to you openly and honestly. I can't do that with many people. No one else, really."

"Not even the crew you work with? You claim they're like brothers to you."

"They are. We'd do anything for each other, and sure, I can talk to them, but not the way I can to you. With you, I feel..." Breaking off, he searched for the right word. "Heard. I'm glad I can trust you, Sarah." A big deal.

She dipped her head. "I'm honored."

"Thanks. Now it's your turn."

After hauling in a breath, she started. "I've been

dreaming a lot about sex, which you already know, and fighting with myself about it for a while now. From the second you showed up earlier and throughout dinner, I've been conflicted. Sex tonight or not? Well, I made a decision about the situationship thing. I'm all in."

The unexpected words blew him away. "Seriously? I thought you wanted to slow down. Like I said, we can wait, no pressure. I'm a patient guy."

"Well, I'm impatient. I need sex, and I need it with you. Tonight."

"Got it." He grinned, then thought about it and sobered. "Sex can change things, and as I said, I don't want to lose you."

She pursed the lips that obsessed him. "Are you trying to talk me out of making love? I'm about to pop out of my skin with lust for you. You have to get back to Toad later, and time's a-wastin.'" She held out her hand. "Come to bed with me."

Hard to argue with that, and he was all in. But first... "Are you on birth control?"

"I haven't been with a man in forever, but yes. Do you have protection? Are you clean?"

"Affirmative on both. Like you, it's been a few years, but I've been carrying a packet or two in my pocket since you first turned me on. Just in case."

"Smart man. Now, come here and kiss me." She crooked her finger and beckoned him closer.

~

ABOUT TO MAKE love with Daniel at last, Sarah lost herself in passionate kisses that melted her into a pool of desire.

"You're so hot," he murmured, his hands already under her pullover.

"Because I'm burning for you. Undo my bra."

"Maybe we should go to your bedroom first. Is it down the hall?"

"First room on your left." She grasped his hand and hurried toward it.

Moments later, having stripped off their tops, they stared at each other. She noted the scar on his left shoulder and down part of his chest. "Is that from the fire in Sacramento?" He nodded. "Will it hurt if I touch it?"

"Not at all." Careful all the same, she ran her fingers tenderly over the bumpy skin. "That's quite a big scar."

"It was a nasty burn, for sure. Forget about me. I want to look at you." He gazed at her with something like awe. "Such pretty breasts," he murmured, tracing one eager nipple, then the other with his finger.

Pleasure arced through her, and her neediest place ached for attention. "Mmm," she murmured, and stepped in as close as she could. His fevered skin against hers felt like heaven. Wanting to touch him again, she ran her hands over his powerful back. With the exception of the scar, his skin was smooth. "No other burns?"

"The one is enough. I want you naked."

"Bossy man. You, too."

After tossing a condom on one of the bedside tables, Daniel stripped off the rest of his clothes. Sarah followed suit. Moments later, they were both nude. He was muscled, fit, and fully erect—a gorgeous male.

He studied her with what looked like reverence. "You're a goddess, and tonight you're all mine."

Tonight? What about the future? They were in a

situationship and didn't have one, she reminded herself. For an instant, her world darkened. Then he cupped her hips and lifted her, his erection against her crotch. She stopped worrying about what would happen later and fixated on what really mattered—savoring their time together now and enjoying the love play.

He'd called her a goddess, no doubt due to his desire. She wasn't half bad, but certainly not beautiful and nowhere near perfect. "I'm not."

"In my eyes you are." Pulling the covers away, he guided her onto the bed with him.

She lay on her back with her head on her pillow, while he did things to her nipples with his hands and mouth that drove her mad with desire. As she squirmed and pushed upward toward him, he let out a low laugh.

"You weren't kidding about being impatient. We'll get there, okay?" As good as his word, he began to make his way toward her most needy place. Way too slowly. Soon, on the verge of climaxing, she lost patience. "As much as I love what you're doing, I need more," she pleaded, and nipped one of his nipples.

His dark eyes glittered. "When you make up your mind, you mean it—" He shut his mouth as she reached down and slid her palm over his arousal. Groaning, he lifted her hand away. "Forget slow. I need to be inside you. Now."

"Thank goodness. Hurry." She raised up and gripped his firm behind.

Almost as soon as he entered her, an intense orgasm started. She lost herself in waves of pleasure. When it finally ended and he grinned down at her, she felt complete and happy, and for the first time in her life, truly beautiful. "That's some cocky grin," she told him, as he snuggled her closer. "But wow."

"Wow is right. It—*you*—are something special. I'm only cocky because I satisfied you. It happened fast, but I don't think either of us wanted to slow down." He smiled into her eyes. "If I can control myself next time, I'll pleasure you even more. Too bad I have to leave soon. I'll be right back." He scooped his clothes off the floor before padding toward the bathroom.

While he was gone, she luxuriated in the intense gratification filling her. She'd never felt this fantastic during and after sex. None of her previous partners had given her pleasure like Daniel. What an amazing lover he was. What an amazing man, period. Utterly in love with him, she sighed in peace and contentment. It wasn't long before a question intruded. Why did it feel as if she'd just now fallen for Daniel when she'd been in love with him for a while now?

Because something inside her had shifted. Her heart swelled with love and a joy far deeper than she'd ever imagined, so strong, her entire being, body and soul, hummed blissfully.

For the first time in her life, she understood what it felt to put her heart into another person's hands. But Daniel would never feel the same toward her—he'd made sure she understood that Kendall owned his heart.

Yet knowing that, she'd gone ahead and had sex with him. Not the kindest way to treat herself. Her short-lived elation faded, leaving her feeling like a fool. Even so, she wanted to slip into the bathroom and cling to him. But no, she wouldn't let him see her neediness or share her true feelings, ever. It was a good thing he'd be leaving soon—pulling herself together wasn't something she wanted him to see.

As his footsteps announced he was headed back to the bedroom, she hurried from the bed, quickly pulled her robe from the closet, and shrugged into it.

"I like that robe. Bright blue suits you."

"Thanks. I would've put on pajamas, but they're in the bathroom, and I didn't want to impinge on your privacy."

"I wouldn't have minded. If I'd known you wanted them, I'd have brought them to you. Wish I could stay longer. I hope you sleep well. I know I will. Nothing like good sex to relax a person."

This was true—even if she was heartsick inside.

"Here's an idea," he said. "I'll be out running errands tomorrow afternoon, but if you want to come over in the morning..." His eyes got hot again.

She melted, her love for him threatening to spill from her lips and ruin everything. Schooling herself to mask her feelings, she managed a benign mien. "You know I want to, but I have a full day tomorrow—grocery shopping, laundry, and knitting more pieces before the craft fair opens." She silently congratulated herself for not sounding at all needy.

He looked disappointed. "Ah, well, it was worth a try. With my family arriving during my shift Tuesday, we'll have to wait till after Thanksgiving. I'll let myself out. See you at the Hearthstone." He kissed her gently on the lips and left.

As soon as she heard the front door close behind him, she gathered her clothes from the carpet, tossed them in the bathroom hamper, donned her pajamas, and wondered what to do now. Stay involved with Daniel, knowing what they shared wouldn't last? That didn't feel right, but neither did the thought of ending the relationship that meant so much. She returned to the bedroom to sleep, but her emotions and indecision kept her awake. Figuring Erin was still up, she sent a text. *Need to talk. Meet at Rosemary's tomorrow morning for breakfast?*

Immediately, her friend texted back. *Perfect timing—Flick has plans with his guy friends. Let's go early to beat the Sunday brunch crowd.*

Sarah replied with a thumbs up. She fell asleep hugging the pillow where Daniel had rested his head.

18

The following morning, Sarah arrived at Rosemary's before Erin. Although several early risers filled a few tables, the Sunday brunch crowd had yet to appear, and she had her pick of seats. Wanting to share what'd happened with her friend in relative privacy and get her insights, she chose a table for two in the otherwise empty back corner, where they could talk without being overheard.

Minutes later, Erin blew through the door as if the wind had pushed her inside. She went straight to the table. "It sure is getting cold out there. Winter has arrived."

As soon as she sat down, a waitress appeared at the table to fill their mugs with steaming coffee. The day's brunch special posted on the large menu board looked yummy, but in turmoil as she was, Sarah couldn't work up much enthusiasm. She asked for an English muffin.

Erin ordered the special and frowned. "Aren't you hungry?"

"Not yet." Sarah added sugar and cream to her mug.

"Well, I am. I'm sure that soon you'll be, too. You can always order food later. The first coffee of the day is always good, and the food here is a cut above." Erin licked her lips. "You wanted to talk?"

Sarah lowered her voice. "Last night, Daniel suggested we have a situationship—do you know what that is?" when Erin nodded, she went on. "We had sex."

"Now, that's news worth getting up for." Her friend leaned forward. "And?"

"It was wonderful, of course. But not long after, I realized I'd made a mistake. I don't want a situationship, I want a commitment. I'll never have that with him. The other problem is even worse."

Erin looked totally confused. "There's another one?"

"Unfortunately. You already know my feelings for him. I thought I did, too, only I was mistaken." Before she went on, breakfast arrived.

Erin dug in. Sarah spread butter and jam on her muffin but couldn't eat it.

"OMG, this is so good," Erin raved, and eyed Sarah with concern. "You haven't even taken a bite of the muffin. You're really upset, and I'm lost. What do you mean, *mistaken*? Are you saying you don't like him after all because of the commitment issue?"

"Not exactly. This is going to sound crazy, but I love him even more than I thought I did."

"Um, okay." The eating stopped. "I still don't get it."

"I hardly understand myself. All I know is my feelings for him are deeper now, stronger than I ever dreamed they could be. I've never felt like this and wish I didn't now. No matter how much I love him, I can't have sex with him solely out of desire. I don't want to hide what's in my heart, either." Putting her thoughts into words helped shed light on the situation, and suddenly she knew what she had to do. The painful realization brought tears to her eyes, which she quickly blinked away.

Erin was quiet a moment. "I think I get that—you're worried he won't love you back. You've said that from the beginning. It might not be true. You've fallen even harder for him than you ever imagined. Maybe he's falling for you, too, or already has."

If only that were true. "I know he won't—Kendall, remember? Plus, he's totally into this situationship thing. Last night, it was all I could do not to tell him how I felt. I teared up because I just this minute figured out what I have to do." She swallowed. "I can't see him anymore."

"Oh, honey." Erin reached out and squeezed her upper arm in sympathy. "Are you sure?"

"No, but besides banning sex with him, I'll always be on edge, afraid of blurting out my love. That's no way to live."

"I have to agree. He'll want to know why you're breaking up with him. How are you going to answer that?"

"I made the decision less than five minutes ago. Give me a little time to figure it out, okay?"

Erin's sympathetic expression vanished. "Don't take your frustration out on me. I'm trying to help."

Aware she'd sounded mad at her dearest friend, Sarah apologized. "I shouldn't have snapped at you. I know you mean well."

"You're forgiven. I have a hunch you're hangry."

Same thing Daniel had said over dinner the previous night. It'd been true then and also was now.

Sarah took a bite of the muffin. It tasted really good, and she quickly finished the whole thing. Her mood improved a little. "I feel better now. Not great, though, but I think I'll order something to go."

"I would. You can't help but be upset. When are you supposed to see him again?"

"Thanksgiving Day at the Hearthstone. He'll be there with his family, and I'll be with mine. Both sets of parents are eager for us to meet someone and settle down. We don't want them to have even an inkling we're involved. If we happen to run into each other, we'll say hello and play it cool, like acquaintances. His family won't be in town long, and Mason and Lee are going on their cruise, so it's likely they'll forget about imagining the two of us together.

"I know I have to break things off soon, but I'll be busy getting ready for the craft fair next weekend, and I won't be able to tell him right away. With both of us working, I'm not sure when I'll see him, let alone end it." She dreaded the thought. "It has to be done, though."

"Okay, but as you say, you decided mere minutes ago. You made up your mind pretty fast. If it were me, I'd sit on the decision a while before doing anything."

Sarah agreed. "I guess I do sound impulsive. It won't hurt me to wait awhile."

"Just don't do it on Thanksgiving."

"Ruin the holiday for him? I won't. But with my self-esteem at stake, I don't see how I can possibly change my mind."

"Atta girl—hold onto that self-esteem you've worked so hard on. Flick and I leave for Tucson after work Wednesday. I'll be back Monday, but you can always text or call if you need to."

Bother her over the long weekend? Doubtful. "I'll

keep that in mind, but I'll be busy working and probably won't be able to talk to Daniel till you're back."

Breakfast was over. Sarah's takeout arrived all boxed up, and they exited the café. Outside, they hugged each other and went their separate ways.

~

THAT SAME MORNING, Daniel headed to the grocery to pick up snacks and treats for his family. They wouldn't be staying with him, but they'd no doubt want to see his place. He planned to be ready with food and a clean apartment. While he shopped, he thought about Sarah and the previous night with her. He wanted that again.

After bringing the food home, he decided cleaning could wait. Restless, he headed to Upton's Gym, which wasn't far from where he lived, to play basketball with whoever showed up. For a Sunday, there weren't too many competitors, but enough to play hard and work up a sweat. In the locker room sometime later, while he splashed his hot face with cold water before driving home, Tony sauntered in.

"Hey, man," he greeted Daniel.

"Hey." Daniel frowned. "What're you doing here? This is quite a drive from your place."

"Summer says I hover too much and told me to find something else to do. I could've gone running with Boomer, but it's awful cold today." He shrugged. "I like this gym and I'm in the mood to shoot hoops."

"Too bad you didn't come earlier. I'm about to take off. How is Summer?"

"Getting antsy about the baby. She's due next month."

"That explains the hover comment. Like you, I needed exercise and wasn't about to spend it outside."

"Still seeing Sarah?'

No reason to deny it. Daniel nodded.

"That's some big, honkin' grin. Things must be going well."

"Real well." He could hardly wait to see her again.

"Are you sleeping with her?"

"None of your business."

"You are. Way to go." Tony gave him a knowing look. "You're half in love with her, am I right?"

More like lust. Daniel shook his head. "I like her a lot, but I don't love her." He wasn't ready for that.

"You remind me of myself when Summer and I first got together. It took time for us to figure out we loved each other."

Enough conversation already. "It's lunchtime and I'm hungry, plus I need to clean my place before the family shows up."

"That's right. When do they arrive?"

"At some point Tuesday afternoon—they decided to drive up, but no idea what time. The six of them want to visit the firehouse after dinner that night."

"Six. Wow."

"Don't I know it. Besides my folks, my sister and her husband and two boys are coming."

"Cool. Your place is too small to host all those people. Where will they bunk?"

"They booked rooms at the Willard Motel, which I guess is near Guff's Lake Resort. I looked up the place, and the reviews are okay. I hope they'll be comfortable. Do you know anyone who's stayed there?"

"No, but if it's near the resort, I'm guessing lots of tourists do. It won't be four-star, but decent. What about Thanksgiving?"

"Believe it or not, my folks got reservations at the Hearthstone for that. It's less than a mile from the motel."

Tony whistled. "Swanky restaurant for Thanksgiving. I gotta ask—will Sarah be with you?"

"That's a good question." Looking perplexed, Tony scratched his head, and Daniel explained. "It's kinda strange—her parents are leaving town the day after and they also made a reservation at the Hearthstone." The guy's eyes almost bugged out of his head. "Don't go getting any ideas—the families don't know each other. Plus, the place will be packed. Chances are, she and I won't run into each other, which is fine."

"If it were me, I'd want to be with my woman and let the world know she was mine."

"I'm not you and she's not my woman, okay?" Daniel's stomach rumbled impatiently. "Like I said, I'm hungry and need a shower. I want to hang out with Toad for a while, too, before I drop him at Jenny's." With the shift starting at eight a.m. and breakfast with the crew prior to that, most of his teammates who boarded their dogs with her dropped them off Sunday night. "See ya."

Tony headed to the basketball court, and Daniel drove home. He cleaned his place, which mostly meant vacuuming and tidying up, then took a long, hot shower and fantasized about him and Sarah making love under the shower spray. Have to try that soon. Later, after dinner and dropping off Toad, he drove toward his place.

It was hard not to stop by Sarah's, but they both had to be up early. At home again, he phoned her for no reason at all. The phone rang for a while before voicemail clicked on. "Hey," he said. "I've been thinking about you. Last night was great. Holding you in my arms, making you get all squirmy and ready..." He groaned, and realized he was turned on again. Basketball game aside, it'd been this way all day. He cleared his throat. "Okay, that's enough. Here's to a great day tomorrow, and see you at the Hearthstone. Night."

19

It took a great deal of will power for Sarah not to answer when Daniel phoned. She heard the message, though, and when he disconnected, played it several more times. Which was torture because she wanted so much to talk to him. Feeling the way she did, how could she possibly break things off? By everything he said, it was painfully obvious that although he liked her, sex was foremost on his mind. She was in the same boat, except she loved him. Too bad he didn't feel that way, but then, he'd been honest from the start.

She hadn't changed her mind—the only choice was to end things as soon as possible. Sick at heart, she erased the message and cried.

Over the next few days, work kept her busy. When her shift ended Tuesday afternoon, she took Puff to the Animal Care Clinic for her after-spay checkup. Dr. Gruen pronounced her healed enough to remove the onesie. Sarah was thrilled, and so was Puff. Free of the thing made the kitty happy and more playful that evening, and Sarah smiled and even laughed a time or two over her funny antics. A boost to her low spirits.

She thought about messaging Daniel about that,

but didn't. No sense starting a conversation which could lead to more pain. He didn't contact her, either. Likely getting ready to see his family, who were due in town that very day. For all she knew, they were already there. As curious as she was about them, steering clear of them and him seemed best.

DURING BREAKFAST at the firehouse Monday, the team shared their various Thanksgiving plans. Most of them had family or friends to spend the holiday with. "Wait'll you hear what Daniel's doing," Tony said and nodded at him to explain.

The guys got quiet, their attention on him. *Brother.* He narrowed his eyes at Tony to shut his big mouth. Naturally, that didn't faze the dude. "You all know my family will be here for Thanksgiving," he reminded them. "They should arrive tomorrow afternoon and plan to stop by for a tour, probably early evening. As far as Thanksgiving goes, we're eating at the Hearthstone. Satisfied, Tony?"

"Not quite. Tell them about Sarah's plans."

Daniel regretted ever mentioning that at the gym. "What the hell difference does it make?" he grumbled. "It's no big deal. Apparently, her parents made reservations at the same place and in the same time slot. It wasn't planned—they don't know each other—just happened. That's it."

Tony's smirk irritated him no end, and he ignored it. "I should add that if you meet my relatives when they visit tomorrow, don't mention Sarah or that we'll be at the same place Thanksgiving. It'll be crowded in there and we may not see each other, plus I don't want my mother on my case about her." He level-eyed Tony. "We're done here."

Without another word about it, the team finished breakfast and started the daily chores.

The rest of Monday and most of Tuesday were more or less routine, with several paramedic calls, a handful of low-level fires, and the never-ending chores. He heard nothing from Sarah, but like him she was busy. When she announced emergencies, he pictured her serious and intent on her work and smiled to himself about the passionate woman underneath.

Tuesday afternoon, his mom texted to let him know they'd checked into their motel and were on their way to dinner. When they finished, they'd head for the firehouse. Looking forward to that but also on edge—twoplus years had passed, and things were sure to be uncomfortable—he joined his teammates for dinner. After the meal, he thought about phoning Sarah. Her shift had ended a while ago, and she was probably at home. He was about to contact her when the family arrived.

His mom looked him over, sniffled, and gave him a big hug. "It's so good to see you, Daniel. You look wonderful."

He regretted not reaching out more often. "Thanks, Mom. You look great yourself." Trim and pretty. "Are you crying?"

"Tears of joy. I've missed you so much."

"All of us have." His dad, who was roughly the same height as him, clapped his shoulder. "I'm awful glad to see you, Son."

"My turn," said his sister Izzy, blonde like their mom and several inches taller. They exchanged big hugs. Her husband Cyrus gave him a one-arm bro hug. "Happy to see you, Daniel."

Last to greet him were Izzy and Cyrus's kids, eight-year-old Lucas and his six-year-old brother Aiden. Not wanting to tower over the two, Daniel hunkered down to greet them. They barely remembered him and were shy at first but when he gave them each kid-size, red firefighter hats, they warmed right up. Suddenly excited and talkative, they bombarded him with questions about his job. He answered as succinctly as possible and promised to show them the firehouse, and yes, let them sit in an actual engine.

"What's the motel like?" he wanted to know as he led them to the lower floor to see the vehicles and equipment.

"It's nice," his mom told him. "Clean and quiet."

"Lucas and I get to share a big bed," Aiden proudly announced.

His big brother narrowed his eyes. "You'd better not wake me up in the night, Aiden."

Behind them, Izzy and Cyrus rolled their eyes. The boys quibbled a bit before Izzy stepped in. "Be nice to your brother, Lucas."

Daniel took them all over the station, introducing them to his friends and Captain Comings, who stopped to talk. Izzy and Daniel's mom seemed as starstruck as the boys, and why wouldn't they be? The forty-five-year-old man was friendly, good-looking, and as buff as the rest of them. Daniel's dad and Cyrus, also visibly impressed, were good-natured about it.

Over the course of the tour, the family met the rest of the team. All in all, it was a good way to spend an evening. When it was time for them to go, they made plans to meet up again after breakfast the following morning, and then explore the park. They also wanted to see his apartment and greet Toad, who'd been a pup when Daniel had relocated.

As soon as they left, he headed upstairs to his bunk, sliding the phone from his pocket on the way, and called Sarah. After several days without any contact, he missed her.

The phone rang several times before she picked up. "Daniel?" She sounded both groggy and worried. "Is everything okay?"

He glanced at his watch and noted it was later than he'd thought. "Shoot, I woke you up. Sorry about that. It's not important."

"I forgot to put my phone on Do Not Disturb. No worries—I'm awake now."

"I won't keep you long. My family just left the firehouse. I gave them a full tour. It was great to see them and start getting to know my nephews, Aiden and Lucas. They were too young to remember me much when I left."

"You sound happy."

He sat back against his pillow and grinned. "I am. Anyway, this seemed a good time to give you some intel about them, insights you might want to know." He pulled in a breath. "Also, I miss you."

"Me, too." Her tone was melancholy.

"You okay?"

"A bit groggy. Tell me about your family."

"Everyone looks good. My parents haven't aged much, but it's only been a few years." Having spent over an hour with them that evening, as limited as the time had been, he realized how much he'd missed them. "My sister and brother-in-law seem content with their busy lives, and are excited to be in town. Lucas and Aiden have grown quite a bit. I gave them firefighter hats they really liked. I don't believe they've been in a fire station before, and they seemed to enjoy the tour. Maybe they'll be firefighters themselves someday. They're going to be tall."

"Like you."

"I think so. They look at me like I'm a hero." Seeing himself through their eyes had made him feel proud.

"You are."

"Just doing my job."

"H

phoned you Sunday night. Did you get my message?"

She hesitated. "I did."

"When I didn't hear back, I wondered."

"That was a busy day, and so was every day since. Besides working, I'm knitting like crazy to make sure I have enough inventory to sell at the craft fair."

He regretted waking her up, but so liked chatting with her. "Nice talking to you tonight. I'll let you get back to sleep now."

"Okay."

She wanted off the phone. He understood. Yet he also sensed something underneath, a distance that bothered him. Had something changed? Nah, he assured himself. Between getting things done before Thanksgiving and the holiday fair, she was stressed. He didn't blame her. "That's it for now. See you Thursday—maybe."

"Goodnight." She disconnected.

20

Thanksgiving day, Sarah woke up early, already a bundle of nerves. Daniel's call the other night had ripped her open. She didn't want to break up with him, but the fear of blurting out her feelings made ending things a must. "I'll tell him after Thanksgiving," she informed Puff over breakfast. Content after her morning meal, the kitten was busy playing with the toy mouse Daniel had given her. The squeaky thing was one of her favorite amusements.

The reservation at the Hearthstone was for one o'clock, her mother had reminded her in a text the previous evening. Which she already knew. She preferred not to see Daniel, but if she did...she had no idea what to do, except play the part of a casual friend.

Her brother Elton had offered to drive and showed up shortly after noon. Besides being three years younger and a few inches taller than she was, he had thick hair she envied. They shared the same hazel eyes. The instant she let him in, Puff dashed under the couch, so fast, he didn't see her. "That's a pretty dress," he said.

"It's fun to wear clothes a step above business casual now and then. You did, too, I see. You look so handsome."

"Thanks. Lee said not to wear jeans and to put on a nice shirt, so I bought a wool pullover and these pants." He looked around. "Where's the kitty?"

"Hiding under the couch. Come out, Puff," she coaxed. "Elton's nice—he wants to meet you." No response, and she gave her brother a what-can-you-do? look. Such a different reaction from when Daniel was here, but then, he'd rescued her from a tree. "Maybe next time."

She didn't see or talk to Elton often, and on the drive to the resort they caught up. "How's work?" she asked. Her brother was a scheduler at Lucky Joe's, a wildly popular venue for music and other programs.

"Hectic. Making sure all holiday events are ready to go isn't as easy as it seems. It'll be good to have tomorrow off. A four-day weekend." He grinned. I'm seeing a girl, but I'm not ready to tell Lee or Mason."

"You can tell me, though. Who is she?"

"Her name's Mikey, and she's a pharmacist at a drugstore near the fire station. I met her when my buddy Austen had a prescription filled there."

"Interesting way to meet. How long have you been seeing each other?"

"A few months. What about you, Sarah? Any guys in your life?"

Tell her brother or not? She decided she would. "Yeah, but I don't think it'll last." Amazing how normal she sounded. "Like you, I don't want our parents sniffing around my dating life."

"No problem. So you don't like him much."

"I do, but it's one-sided." She swallowed back a sob. "Funny thing—he and his family are having

Thanksgiving at the Hearthstone at the same time as we are. I hope I don't run into him."

"If you do, Lee and Mason will be all over you."

"Not if I can help it. He doesn't want his family getting any ideas, either, and we've agreed to keep our business private."

Finding a place to park was no picnic, but Elton finally edged into a space—right beside a RAV4 that looked a lot like Daniel's. He wasn't the only person in town to own one, but by the dog harness in the back seat, the car was his. Her wayward heart lifted, darn it. The thought of seeing him and pretending she was fine when she was anything but wouldn't be easy. She wanted to turn around and go home, but of course couldn't. *Stay calm and cool*, she silently counseled herself.

Minutes later, she and Elton headed toward the entrance of the resort.

DANIEL HAD NEVER BEEN to the Hearthstone. It was as upscale as he'd imagined: linen tablecloths, plush carpeting, and fresh autumn flowers in small vases on each table. The restaurant was crowded, but thanks to high-quality soundproofing fairly quiet, which set a tone of intimacy. As the hostess led them to a table reserved for the family, he noted scattered empty tables reserved for other diners. Which one was for Sarah's family? Soon enough, he'd find out.

Having waited for the midday meal after small breakfasts, both his nephews were hungry and eager to eat. From where Daniel sat, he had a view of the entrance to the restaurant. While he chatted with the boys and the rest of the family, he kept a watchful eye out for Sarah. When she failed to come in, he figured her family had been put in the spillover room set up for the overflow and that he was unlikely to see her. He was both relieved—he wouldn't have to keep a lid on his feelings—and disappointed.

Moments later, when he spotted her mom, Lee, enter the room with a man who had to be her husband, he realized Sarah could be in close proximity. The hostess led them toward a table on the other side of the room. Wait'll Sarah discovered they were within sight of each other. On the way, Lee stopped to greet him.

She was dressed in stilettos and a clingy dress. "Hi, Daniel. I'm Lee from the spa."

"I remember you. These are my parents and my sister, brother-in-law, and nephews." He shared their names to nods and smiles.

So did Lee. "Nice to meet you all. This is my husband, Mason." Mason greeted the group, and Lee went on. "I work at Massage Plus Spa here in the resort. Several weeks ago, Daniel taught a wonderful class on safety preparedness. He's an excellent teacher."

"Is that right?" His mother glanced at him with pride. "I wish we'd sat in on that, but we live in Sacramento and are only here through Saturday."

Mason glanced around. "Sarah and Elton should be along shortly—we should get to our table, hon. Enjoy your visit."

"So she was in a class you taught," his mom commented, her mouth quirking. "She certainly looked you over, but I suspect most women do." Slightly embarrassed, Daniel brushed the comment off. "She mentioned Sarah and Elton. I'll bet they're her kids."

"They are, but I only know Sarah. She's one of the

dispatchers and the main person to alert us to emergencies and where they are."

A male server stopped at the table with water and took orders for cocktails and mocktails for the boys, then left to place the drinks order and attend to other diners. The upcoming meal would be the same for everyone with the exception of a non-meat dish for vegetarians in place of turkey.

As they sipped their drinks, other locals stopped by the table to greet Daniel. His family were impressed that so many people knew him. A sixth sense told him when Sarah arrived. In a pretty dark-green dress that gently draped her curves, she looked beautiful. The male she was with had to be her brother. They seemed tight and were involved in an animated conversation Daniel envied. Prior to losing Kendall, he and Izzy had been close like that. Maybe they could be again.

Sarah glanced his way. When she spotted him, she visibly sucked in a breath. Not that he could hear it. After shooting him a warning look, she glanced in the direction of the hostess as if she didn't notice him. Talk about playing the casual thing to the hilt. When she and her brother reached their parents' table, her mother pointed at Daniel. He nodded and offered a casual wave in return. Sarah did the same. He wanted to head for the other table and greet her with a brief kiss, but wasn't about to fuel any curiosity from the parents. The way to avoid that was to dial his feelings way back.

When he returned his attention to his own table, his mother and sister both looked at him with blatant curiosity.

"Those two must be Lee and Mason's adult kids," Izzy said. "Do you know them?"

"I know Sarah but haven't met her brother. She's the dispatcher for the firehouse."

"She's cute."

Like he hadn't noticed. Lucky for him, the server arrived with drinks and a basket of piping hot appetizers. The boys, who were starving, wolfed down several. Knowing a feast was coming soon, everyone else held back.

"Don't you want to stop at her table and say hi to the family like her mother did us?" his mom suggested.

Already pushing on him when he and Sarah had exchanged casual waves at each other? The best response was to not react. "There's no need. She's with her family, and I'm with mine."

Despite his intentions, pretending he wasn't interested in her proved impossible. He glanced at her table way too often. Caught her looking at him, too. Each time, she bit her lip and looked away. He was right there with her, wanting to be together but pretending otherwise. Who cared if the families figured it out? Sarah did. He'd thought he did, too, but he was no longer interested in the charade. He needed to talk to her about that, and soon.

"Why do you keep staring at that lady?" Aiden wanted to know.

Daniel started to deny that he was, but the adults at the table had also noticed. He didn't want to say anything until he talked to her. He thought fast. "Besides me, she's the only person from the station here —that's why." Which was no reason at all.

The first course arrived and the conversation turned to the incredible salad, excitement for the next course, and other small talk. Any time now, the turkey and sides would arrive. At that moment, Sarah stood and headed toward the entrance without looking his way. The perfect time for that talk. After a few seconds, he slid his chair away from the table and stood. "I'll be right back."

21

The two cocktails Sarah had enjoyed before the Thanksgiving meal were supposed to help her relax and did. She also felt slightly tipsy, which messed with her common sense. Case in point, boldly staring across the room at Daniel more than once. He seemed to be having a good time with his family. While she was happy for him, she was also envious. Her own family rarely enjoyed each other like that.

More than once, she caught him glancing at her, too. Each time, her stomach clenched and her heart contracted. Knowing she had to end things with him hurt and made for the most stressful Thanksgiving of her life.

"You keep looking at Daniel," Lee commented with a shrewd expression.

Darn her for noticing. "It's not him I'm focused on," she fibbed, but only a little. "His family interests me. Those young boys are so cute. From what I can tell, they keep the entire group in stitches." Even Daniel. She'd never seen him so lighthearted. "It's fun to watch." She noted the server headed their way. "Oh, good, the salads are here. I'm starving, and I need food. I should never drink on an empty stomach."

Ready to take a break from faking a lightheartedness she didn't feel, she finished the salad and decided to find the bathroom. At least there she wouldn't be able to catch sight of Daniel. He was difficult to resist, and seeing him weakened her resolve to break things off. She needed space to collect herself, and the ladies' room seemed the perfect place. "Excuse me," she said, and headed out of the dining room.

With the opening of the holiday craft fair tomorrow and running through the weekend, there simply wasn't time to break up. Especially today. No sense getting all worked up about it now, she told herself in the silence of the empty bathroom. But the whole idea brought tears to her eyes.

After taking care of business and resolving to end things sometime the following week, she glanced at her reflection and winced. Her cheeks were way too pink, which sometimes happened when she imbibed. She touched up her makeup. That helped. Her hair needed fixing, too.

While she worked on that, a startling thought popped into her head. Erin said Daniel wouldn't treat her to meals and spend time with her unless she was more than a friend. What if it were true but for some reason he hadn't told her? Maybe he needed a push after all. But no, he wanted a situationship.

Her stomach growled, a reminder she needed more food. Any time now, the main meal would arrive. Eager to eat, she exited the bathroom.

To her surprise, Daniel stood in the hallway, giving her the warm look that made her insides go all soft. Such a handsome, irresistible man. She stared up at him, her resolve growing weaker by the second. "Hi. Why are you lurking outside the Ladies' room?"

"Waiting for you. Seeing you but not being able to relax and be ourselves—we should talk. Alone."

"Where would we do that?" And to what purpose? "This place is packed."

"While you were in the bathroom, I looked around," he said and gestured at a hallway. "There's an empty room down there, and the door's unlocked."

Be alone with him now, when she felt so needy and lovesick? She panicked. "I don't think we should. I feel woozy from the cocktails I drank, and I need food—"

"This won't take long, I promise. Come inside for a minute."

She sighed and gave in. As soon as he shut the door, he pulled her close and kissed her. She started to melt, then came to her senses and pushed him away. "Don't."

He released her. "Wrong time, wrong place, I know. I wanted so much to kiss you, I couldn't help myself. That should tide me over. Now we can talk."

"What's so important it can't wait?"

"I'm rethinking this we-hardly-know-each-other phony act. I don't want to play that game anymore. Who cares if people know we're seeing each other?"

Had his feelings about their relationship changed? A thrill ran through her. "Ah, you want something more serious," she guessed, crossing her fingers.

But he looked confused. "I'm saying I want us to be ourselves and put our relationship out there instead of hiding it."

Did his idea of a relationship include a possible future or not? She wasn't about to ask. There was no need—if he wanted that, he'd say so. Face it, he didn't care as deeply about her as she did him. Of course not. Kendall was his number one. "Don't look at me like that, Daniel." Like he wanted to devour her. Not because he loved her, because he desired her physically. It wasn't enough. Refusing to make a needy fool of herself yet again, she stepped away. "I can't."

"Can't what?"

Have sex again without a commitment and hope for a future. "Talk to you now. I have to get back to my family, and so do you."

"Don't leave me hanging. At least give me a hint."

On Thanksgiving Day, in this very public space? "Not here."

"Okay. Why don't I come over later tonight?"

How she wanted that. "I have to be up early for the holiday fair," she said, avoiding his hot eyes.

"That's right. We're both busy. Let's get together next week."

Did he have to be so sweet and understanding?

Radiating concern, he wiped away the tears that had fallen unbidden down her cheeks. "You're crying. What's wrong?"

Damn her traitorous tear ducts. "I—" Afraid of blurting out what she didn't dare admit, she covered her mouth with her hand.

Now he looked alarmed. "Is someone in your family sick? Tell me it isn't you."

She was sick, all right—lovesick for him. "It's nothing like that."

He let out a relieved breath. "That's good to know. No matter what the problem is, I'm here for you. After all the stuff I've dumped on you, that's only fair. Talk to me, Sarah."

The need to fall into his arms and do exactly that

panicked her. "I have to get back to my family." She pivoted away and fled.

WHEN SARAH RETURNED to the table, she worked hard to pretend all was well. But with Lee, Mason, and Elton all scrutinizing her, that wasn't so easy. Her mother opened her mouth to say who knew what, but Sarah stopped her. "Here's our dinner. Sure looks good." It did, even if at the moment she didn't feel like eating. She faked it anyway. Everything was delicious, and she managed to get several bites down. She was debating how much more she could manage when her mother spoke.

"This food is divine and you claim you're hungry, yet you've barely eaten anything. I suspect your sudden loss of appetite has something to do with Daniel. The way you two have been staring at each other, it has to be. He left the dining room shortly after you did and came back a few minutes behind you. He isn't laughing the way he was, either. What happened?"

She would notice all that. As tempted as Sarah was to glance at him, she resisted. "I don't want to talk about it, okay?"

"So it is about him. I knew it."

To Sarah's horror, fresh tears gathered behind her eyes. She blinked hard at her plate, but didn't fool anyone at the table.

Elton placed a comforting hand on her shoulder. "Stop it, Mom."

"She's my daughter and your sister, and—"

"You heard both Sarah and Elton—leave her alone," Mason warned, and Lee shut her mouth.

Sarah sent a silent thank-you to her mother's husband. "Don't worry about my appetite. I'm not wasting a single bite of this food. I'll take the leftovers and dessert home with me. I think I'll leave now. I'll be up early tomorrow to set up my booth at the holiday craft fair and still need to organize a few things for that." Amazing how calm she sounded when she could barely hold herself together. She really needed Erin, even if it was Thanksgiving and her friend was out of town. "I'll call an Uber, Elton, so you don't have to leave."

Her brother shook his head. "No way—I'm taking you home. I'm too full for dessert just yet, but I'll bring it with me."

Mason nodded. He signaled a server and directed him to box up Sarah's dinner and two desserts.

"Thank you both for tonight," she said, again, her voice trembling slightly despite herself. "This was really nice. Enjoy your cruise, and please send updates and photos."

"We will," Mason said.

Lee nodded, her lips curled into a frown. "I don't know what you're going through, Sarah, but I see how upset you are. I wish I knew, but you don't talk to me. Neither do you, Elton." Sarah swore her mother was hurt. Maybe someday they'd talk about the gaping hole between them. "I'm here for you any time. I love you, honey, and so does Mason."

On the verge of totally losing it, Sarah pulled herself together through sheer grit. "I know, Mom, and I appreciate that. Maybe later." As she retrieved her coat, she stole a glimpse at the man she loved. He was focused on his food and seemed as subdued as she was, which didn't make her feel any better. The day hadn't turned out so well, but at least she hadn't ended things on Thanksgiving Day.

22

Minutes after Sarah returned to the dining room, Daniel made his way through the Hearthstone to rejoin his family. He registered the clinks of silverware, laughter, and conversation with dread. She'd pulled away just as he'd sensed the other night when he'd phoned her. At that time he'd brushed off the feeling, but this afternoon there was little doubt that something between them had gone wrong. She hadn't so much as hinted at what the problem was, but it'd been a bad time to talk.

The queasy feeling in his gut signaled bad news. He knew it wasn't health-related. Maybe she had doubts about seeing him anymore. She'd said something like that before. Yet he knew she liked him as much as he liked her. Kissing her in the deserted room down the hall had been as sweet as ever. Shortly after and without warming, her warmth had faded. She wanted to break up—that had to be it. What other reason would she have for tearing up and disengaging?

Damn, that stung.

He stumbled back to the dining room. Somehow, he had to get through the meal and hang with the family until they went back to their motel. Refusing to look in the direction of her table, he composed himself and returned to his seat. His sister frowned. "You don't look so good. Please don't be getting sick."

"I'm okay—just need to eat." Untrue, but he didn't want to put a damper on what had started out as an enjoyable family Thanksgiving. As soon as he sat down, the server delivered the food. It looked and smelled delicious. Despite his inner turmoil, his belly was empty. So he ate. But working up any enthusiasm was impossible. To his relief, no one noticed—too busy eating and singing praises about the meal. Even the boys.

"I wonder what happened to Sarah," Daniel's mother commented sometime later.

She would mention Sarah. He'd ignored her table during the meal, but turned his head toward it now. She wasn't there. Neither was her brother, and her parents were paying the bill.

"The holiday craft fair opens tomorrow, and she has a booth there," he explained, hiding his rotten feelings. "There's a lot to do to get ready for that." Figuring the explanation put an end to the conversation, he returned his attention to the server headed toward them with a tray of desserts. "Look what's coming our way."

For a few minutes everyone was quiet, enjoying the last dish of the feast. Before long, his mom spoke. "You never mentioned a craft fair. I love to shop those things. Wouldn't it be fun to go?"

Run into Sarah? No, thanks. Wishing he'd kept his big mouth shut, he made an excuse to steer clear. "I don't know—it's gonna be crowded. If you want to shop in town, there are some great stores on Main

Street." Which was sure to be just as crowded, but no need to say so.

His mother pulled a face. "You don't want to go?"

"Not really. Wandering around, looking for stuff to buy isn't my thing."

"Well, it's mine. Does anyone else want to come with me?"

The males at the table shook their heads, but Izzy indicated she was in. "You guys need to find something to do while we're gone."

Cyrus and Daniel's father looked to him. "Any ideas?"

Daniel was in no mood to do much, but his family had come all this way, and tomorrow was their last day in town. Spending more time with his dad, Cyrus, and his nephews would be fun. "Grab a bite, then see a movie?" he suggested. "Several new holiday films debut tonight and will stick around through the holidays. Let's find something Aiden and Lucas will enjoy."

The boys lit up. "Can we get popcorn, too, Uncle Daniel?"

Uncle Daniel. He liked the sound of that. "If your parents okay it."

"Sounds good to me," Cyrus said, and Daniel's dad seconded that.

They agreed to check the movie listings and touch base in the morning. Daniel was more than ready to leave, and as soon as they paid the bill, he stood. "This was fun, but Toad is at home waiting for me."

"Give him some love from us," Izzy said.

"I will." Looking forward to being by himself without pretending everything was fine, yet also dreading the evening of solitude ahead, he took off.

~

"I DIDN'T MEAN to drag you away from the table, and just when dessert was served," Sarah said, as she and Elton exited the restaurant and headed outside through the resort's entry. Their breaths clouding in the cold air, they quickly made their way toward his car.

"Hey, I'm glad you did. Mikey's family is eating right about now, and I'm picking her up after."

"Then I'm not sorry at all for wanting to leave. What are your plans for tonight?"

"I don't know yet. Which reminds me—I need to get hold of her. Would you mind waiting while I give her a call? I'll unlock the car and you can wait for me there."

"Okay." While her brother was on the phone with his girlfriend, she settled into the passenger seat and texted her bestie about talking if possible that evening. Almost immediately, Erin replied she'd get in touch later that night. A big relief.

Moments later, Elton climbed into the driver's seat. "Mikey wants to see a movie tonight, then go out for a light dinner. She'll stay at my place." He grinned.

Sarah envied him for the evening ahead. "Sounds like a great time."

Not that she'd lack for something to do, although it wouldn't be nearly as enjoyable as what her brother had planned. She hadn't finished labeling the last of the boxes of knitting and needed to pack them and the rest into the Honda tonight. That and lamenting to Erin. "Are you two getting serious?"

"Starting to."

"I don't blame you for keeping your feelings to

yourself until you're ready to share your relationship with the world."

Daniel had wanted to get her okay to be open about seeing each other, a good idea. Too bad it had nothing to do with a more serious relationship. After that, the conversation had devolved. She wanted to blame the Thanksgiving holiday and the Hearthstone for having no place to go for a private conversation, but the fault lay with her. Looking back, she cringed. Had she actually cried? His kindness and confusion only added to her remorse. Regretting the whole thing, she swallowed hard.

Elton must've heard that swallow—before easing his car out of the parking slot, he glanced at her. "Hate to break it to you, but Lee already figured out you're into Daniel. You're pretty easy to read."

She grimaced. "I'm not the best at hiding my feelings, especially when I'm upset."

"You aren't the only one. He didn't look so good, either."

Feeling awful, she let out an agonized groan and slapped her forehead with her palm.

"It sucks that you're both suffering," Elton said. "I'm here if you want to talk."

Sarah felt too raw and hurt to explain. "I can't right now."

"No pressure. Why don't you put on some music and I'll get you home."

As soon as they left the parking lot, she broke down. "Changed my mind—I do want to talk about it," she said, unable to suppress an anguished sob.

Elton's dismay was obvious. "Don't cry, Sarah. It's upsetting."

"You think I want to?" Sternly ordering herself to

get a grip, she sniffled and blew her nose. "Is that better?"

Her brother nodded. "He ended things, huh? On the way to the Hearthstone, you said you're into him but he isn't into you."

"I know he likes me. When I came out of the bathroom earlier, he was there waiting for me. He wanted a little time alone together. But I—I couldn't bear that."

"What? You're not making any sense."

"We just talked about how hard it is for me to hide my feelings. The truth is, I'm afraid I'll blurt out the L word and humiliate myself."

"I've been there, and what a train wreck," Elton admitted, surprising her. "A while back, I had this girl-friend I was super into. I thought she felt the same about me. Wrong. After I spilled my guts, she ended things."

Sarah felt for him. "That's exactly what Daniel would do. How did you handle it?"

"Besides acting like an idiot, I moped around for a while. Then I got sick of myself and moved on."

Having spent quite a while doing the same after Jensen, she understood all too well. "That happened with my last boyfriend. I learned my lesson and refuse to let it happen ever again. I'm so mad at myself for ever getting involved with Daniel."

"Ah, you're finally making sense."

"How long did it take before you stopped hurting?" she asked.

"A long time—almost a year. You, with the former boyfriend?"

"About the same. Were you humiliated, too?"

"So bad."

She angled her head his way. "You never said anything."

"I didn't see the point. You didn't clue me in, either."

"Would you mind if I vent about Lee?" She didn't wait for her brother's reply. "What is it about her that makes me feel so less-than and needy? I used to long for a mother who cared about me and what I thought and felt. You know how that worked out. She never had the time or the interest in asking me about any of that stuff. I think that's one reason why I've always rushed into relationships hoping to find love. Now, when she's all interested, I'm not sure I want to talk to her. But for some crazy reason, I feel guilty about that."

"It's complicated, all right," Elton said. You're not the only one who suffered."

"You, too? I never realized, but then, neither of us ever brought it up."

"I never thought to."

"Right? I suppose I have to talk to Lee about Daniel, and I dread that," Sarah said, and exhaled loudly.

"Or not. You told her maybe later, but that doesn't mean you owe her an explanation about anything. She and Mason leave in the morning. They'll be gone two weeks. By then, she may have forgotten."

"As if. You know her better than that. It's midafternoon and she has the rest of the day and tonight to pressure me." She thought a minute. "Maybe I should tell her and Mason the truth and get it over with."

"If you do, she'll want to strangle Daniel."

"This isn't his fault. He told me multiple times he wasn't ready to get serious. Thick-headed me hoped he would anyway, but there's not much chance of that. He's still in love with his wife."

Elton gaped at her. "He's married?"

"Not anymore. She died a few years ago in a car accident."

"Competing with a dead woman? That's gotta be tough." He was silent for a moment, then added, "Lee has always been difficult to get closer to. Maybe you can change your relationship with her."

Sarah pondered the idea. "You mean open up to her about her and my relationship and see what happens? It's worth a try, and if I get rejected, well, it's not the first time. You and I should both work on that. Something to think about. I'm glad we're talking openly for once. I feel closer to you than I have in years."

Elton smiled. "Me, too. I like it, too. We should do this more often. He pulled up to the house. "If you want, I can come in."

"I appreciate that, but I really have a lot to do. Don't worry about me—I'll be fine," she added, and clung to those words.

23

———

"I hope I didn't wake you," Erin said, when she phoned Sarah late Thursday night.

Relieved to hear from her at last, she hurried to assure her closest friend. "If I'd been in bed, I'd have silenced my phone. Right now, I couldn't sleep if I tried."

"I'm intrigued and dying to know everything. How did it go at the Hearthstone? Did you and Daniel run into each other, and what happened with the families?"

Not wanting to bore her with too many details, Sarah summarized. "We did okay at first. Our tables were only a glance away—kinda hard for Daniel and me to ignore each other. Early on, I headed to the bathroom down the hall from the restaurant. When I came out, he was waiting for me."

"Ooh, I'm getting excited."

"Don't bother." Forget the summary. The full story spilled out. When she got to the part about him repeating that he didn't want anything serious, her voice wobbled, but at least she didn't cry. "Silly me had gotten my hopes up. After that, we ran out of time and had to get back to our families. Now you know what happened."

"I'm sorry for your pain, sweetie. So you stuck to your decision and broke up with him? That must've hurt so much. I'm not surprised, though—at breakfast the other day, you said you had to. But I thought you decided not to go there on Thanksgiving Day. Tell me what you said and how he responded."

Erin had misunderstood, and Sarah quickly set her straight. "I didn't break up with him, not in so many words. I was worried I'd blurt out my real feelings and couldn't bear to watch him walk away. My family was waiting, so I headed back to the dining room."

"Ah, you walked away before he did." Miserable, Sarah nodded. Of course, Erin couldn't see that. "I know the craft fair starts tomorrow and next week is work, but he needs to know as soon as possible," her friend added.

"Right, and he understands we won't be able to talk till sometime next week."

"Good. Promise me when you do, you won't leave him clueless and shaking his head. You're better than that. You owe him an explanation."

And that terrified her. "I will, but I don't know what I'll say. I can't imagine humiliating myself in front of him by admitting that my feelings have grown...It's too scary." The whole idea made her acutely uncomfortable, and she changed the subject. "Enough about me. Tell me about your trip and your Thanksgiving."

Erin launched into what she'd been doing, where she and Flick had eaten, and their beautiful hotel room. "You should see the bathtub—it's big enough for both of us, with spigots all around like a spa. Flick is drawing a bath for us now. And the bed—huge and comfortable. It's so romantic. I wish we could stay longer. Who knows, if we decide to get married, we might honeymoon here. Hold on." After a few seconds of silence, she returned. "The tub is ready. We'll talk again when I get back. Take care, okay? And good luck at the fair tomorrow."

His brain a muddled mess, Daniel arrived home from the Hearthstone and one of the most difficult meals ever. Pretending he was happy and life was great after Sarah had unexpectedly gone cold on him had been no cakewalk. In the end, he hadn't been able to fool his family. Hadn't explained what was wrong, either— couldn't. No point going there if she really was calling it quits.

For now it was good to be alone. "I'm home, Toad," he called out. His furry pal hopped across the floor and greeted him with a joyous *woof* and a wagging tail. "Nice to be loved," he said. By a dog, anyway. He didn't expect Sarah to love him and didn't love her, either. But he liked her a lot. Too bad her feelings had gone the opposite direction.

Anxious to get out of his head and distract himself, he changed clothes and went on a chilly run with Toad. The exercise took his mind off his problems, but as he returned home in the near darkness of the after- noon, they flooded back. Following a shower, he opened a beer and settled on the sofa, ate chips, and browsed the tube. Plenty of holiday movies. He picked a funny one without once cracking a smile and turned it off before it ended.

Despite reviewing the past few weeks, he could

think of nothing he'd done to upset her. They got along really well, and the sex had been the icing on the cake of their special friendship. Come to think of it, the last time they'd spoken something had felt off. At the time, he'd chalked it up to calling too late and waking her. She hadn't said anything then, and he was no mind reader.

Talk about a situationship going wrong.

She'd made the decision to have sex pretty fast, and he'd jumped on board. There was no doubt she'd enjoyed it as much as he did, but rushing into it as quickly as they had...

She had regrets about that. The more he thought about it, the more certain he was.

Damn. They needed to talk, and when they did, that would be the first thing on the table.

He went to bed in a funk. Instead of sleeping in Friday morning, he woke up early. Sometime during the night, he'd had a dream featuring Kendall, but he had no recollection of the details. It'd been a while since he'd last dreamed of her. Strange it'd happened last night.

As he sipped coffee and ate breakfast, he checked movies and times. After choosing two or three likely to appeal to his nephews, he texted the info to Izzy, Cyrus, and cc'd his dad to check out when they were awake. Once they chose something, he'd get the tickets and reserve seats.

He wasn't the only early riser. Cyrus got back to him right away, and he was able to score four decent seats for a matinee. Something to look forward to.

No doubt Sarah was up, too, and likely setting up her booth at the holiday fair. Good thing the fair was held indoors. The weather people predicted a cold, cloudy day, with a slight chance of snow flurries. He wished her luck and wondered if his mom and Izzy would see her. If so, maybe they'd tell him about it. Even a crumb of information would do.

"I'm pathetic," he grumbled to Toad, who licked his hand. "Don't worry, buddy, I'm gonna have a good time the rest of today and the weekend. Promise." If it killed him.

24

Friday morning, Sarah arrived at the Guff's Lake Community Center, eager to set up her booth, joining the rest of the thirty-five or so vendors with food or goods to sell. The fair was due to open at ten o'clock, and she finished setting up early enough to walk through the area, greet sellers she already knew, and meet others. She found a few items for her family and friends. At a booth that sold fun things for animals, she bought several catnip toys for Puff and a clever doggie chew toy she was sure Toad would love.

Provided Daniel accepted it.

The previous night's conversation with Erin was fresh in her mind. She was determined to get together with him sometime in the coming week. Thinking about it made her queasy, but it was only fair to talk to him.

"Fifteen minutes," a woman announced over the PA. Sarah hurried back to her booth for a last check that everything was ready.

The doors opened and shoppers poured in—people of all ages, some with children in tow, and even a pet or two. Several hours later, after selling a decent amount of inventory, she needed a bathroom break and something to eat. She'd kept an eye on things for the woman in the adjacent booth. Now the woman offered to reciprocate. As she locked the cash box and reached for her purse to leave, Daniel's mother and sister showed up. She'd never been introduced, but they'd seen her with her family. Now they were here.

After a furtive glance around—no sign of Daniel, thank goodness—she turned on her sales persona and offered a hospitable greeting. "Welcome to my booth. We weren't introduced at the Hearthstone, but I recognize you. You're Daniel's family. I'm Sarah."

His sister beamed at her. "It's great to meet you. I'm Izzy, and this is our mom."

The older woman offered a warm smile, reminding Sarah of Daniel. "Please, call me Edna."

They exchanged pleasantries, which might not have happened if they'd had any idea of the conversation between her and Daniel the previous day.

"I like this venue—lots of light and space in here and a great craft fair," Izzy said. "How are sales?"

"Brisk. It's a good thing I knitted a ton of wintry things."

"Your work is beautiful," Edna praised. "I love the vibrant colors and your designs."

"Thanks. I haven't had a booth here in a while, but I'm raising money for a family I adopted for Christmas this year and want to make it extra special." She couldn't stop herself from asking, "Where are the rest of the family?"

"You mean the guys. They're at a theater seeing a Christmas movie."

"I'm happy they're not here," Izzy said. "I don't want to feel rushed by my dad, the boys, Cyrus, and Daniel. So far, I've found several nice gifts for them."

"That's great. Are you enjoying your stay in Guff's Lake?"

Edna nodded. "Very much so. We're headed back to Sacramento tomorrow. It's been great spending time with Daniel. He seems so happy, a nice change from when we last saw him. But after you left yesterday, his good mood faded." She studied Sarah as if searching for clues to what had happened. "You didn't look so good when you left, either. I think you two are involved, but something went wrong. Are you all right?"

While Sarah thought of a way to answer that, Izzy looked appalled. "Mom! That's none of your business."

Daniel's mother looked embarrassed. "You're right. I apologize for asking." Sarah nodded—what else could she do?—and the woman continued. "Winters aren't real cold in Sacramento, but those hats are too cute to pass up. I want to get one for each of the boys and the men, and a scarf for myself. Also a few of those cute ornaments for friends."

Sarah didn't relax until they chose their favorites and said their goodbyes. During her break, she mulled over when and how to end things with Daniel. With his family leaving tomorrow and the fair running through Sunday, followed by her dispatch job and his forty-eight-hour shift, the conversation would have to wait until Wednesday. An awfully long time, but that couldn't be helped. She'd text and let him know she wanted to explain—if he'd agree to see her.

~

SATURDAY MORNING, Daniel treated his family to

brunch at Rosemary's before their trip back to Sacramento.

"This has been a wonderful visit," his mom said. "Why don't you come down for Christmas—unless you have to work."

He appreciated the offer. "This year it falls on a Thursday, so yeah, I can do that. On one condition. Stop treating Kendall's death like a taboo subject. Refusing to acknowledge what happened by tiptoeing around it made things worse and is a big reason why I moved up here. If anyone, myself included, feels like mentioning her, it's okay."

After holding in his resentment for so long, getting it off his chest felt freeing. Why had he kept them in the dark all this time? He realized now that Sarah's words weeks ago about the difference between pity and compassion had widened his viewpoint.

The adults in his family traded looks. "We felt helpless," Izzy explained. "We didn't know how to react. Every time her name came up, you either changed the subject or left. It's why we stopped mentioning her and what happened."

That was the reason they'd gone silent? At the time, he hadn't had the bandwidth to understand. "I was a mess. I didn't know what I wanted or needed. I guess I expected you to magically figure it out. How could you, when you had no idea how to deal with the situation and neither did I?" What a dolt he'd been.

Izzy spoke up. "I think it's great we're finally talking about this. From now on, if I'm confused and need clarification, I'll ask questions instead of holding my feelings inside."

"Let's all do that," Daniel said, fully on board. "I still miss Kendall, but I'm in pretty decent shape now." Or would be if Sarah hadn't dumped him. Too bad he couldn't go back in time and slow things down. Somehow, he had to get back into her good graces.

"I'm already excited about Christmas," Izzy said. "Having you there will be wonderful. I've missed you so much."

As she hugged him goodbye, she whispered in his ear. "Mom and I stopped at Sarah's booth. I really like her."

So did he, but he wasn't about to admit it. No point giving anyone ideas unless they straightened things out. "She's good people," he said, doing his best to hide his pain.

Sunday morning, he woke up thinking about her and how to fix things before it was too late—if that was even possible. For a bleak minute his outlook dimmed. Then he remembered the brief kiss that'd been as sweet as ever. It gave him hope.

He'd make it happen. All he needed now was to come up with a way to do that.

They'd agreed to get together during the coming week. Like it or not, he'd have to wait.

25

At breakfast Monday morning, the guys talked about their Thanksgiving celebrations. Rob's news was the best—he and Jenny had decided to get back together. When he told everyone, Daniel and the other guys applauded. "It's good to know you both finally came to your senses," Ethan said, and was joined by echoes of the same sentiment.

"It was cool meeting your family the other night, Daniel," Hank commented some minutes later. "They seem real nice. Those kids sure enjoyed visiting us."

"That they did. I'm glad they came up. They had a good time and invited me to visit them over Christmas. I said I would."

Grins all around and a bunch of "that's great" and "good on you" comments.

"I've never eaten at the Hearthstone on a holiday," Nate said. "Was it as good as what your mama makes, and did you see Sarah there?"

"The place was packed with people, but yeah, we saw each other. As for the meal, nothing beats home-cooked, but the food was stellar." In bad need of advice, Daniel paused to sip his coffee before going on.

"But some of the holiday sucked. We had a chance to talk out of view of the family, and—" Stumbling a moment, he fiddled with his mug, then cut to the chase. "I think she dumped me."

Rob frowned. "You *think*? Did she say she wanted to break up with you or not?"

"Not in so many words—we didn't have much time for a conversation. She was distant and wouldn't look me in the eyes. I like her a lot and was sure she felt the same."

"Something must've happened to upset her."

"I think we had sex too soon."

"Wait—You had sex with her on Thanksgiving Day?"

"Are you nuts? My family was in town and I spent a lot of time with them. The sex thing happened before they arrived. I didn't see her again till the Hearthstone."

Tony scratched his head. "Maybe she was irritated that you didn't get in touch sooner."

"Trust me, I tried. After it happened, we spoke briefly on the phone, but that was it. You know how it is before a holiday—she had a lot on her plate and so did I. By then, she was probably already having regrets about rushing into bed."

Ethan frowned. "You don't know for sure about any of that, though. It was Thanksgiving and the Hearthstone was swarming with people, including her family and yours. Maybe you should cut her a break."

"Wish I knew, man. My gut tells me it's over. I don't want that—she's too important to me." He rubbed his hand across his face.

"That's why you look exhausted—circles under your eyes, your face kinda gray."

The nods and comments around the table proved Ethan wasn't the only one with that opinion. Daniel blew out a breath. "Way to make me feel even worse. I'm at a loss what to do."

Ethan went on. "Was it rushing the sex or something else? Find out—then you can figure out your next move."

The entire crew nodded in agreement. "I'm planning to text her shortly and set up a time Wednesday when we're both off." Other than detailing a car that morning, he was free the rest of the day.

Breakfast ended, and the team headed off to tackle the morning chores.

Later, shortly after a call that ended as a false alarm, Daniel texted Sarah, reminding her that they'd agreed to talk. She replied right away. *Sounds good. Why don't I come over in the morning?*

Not the afternoon, then. He texted her back. *I'm leaving at 10:30 to detail a car, but feel free to come before then.*

When the forty-eight-hour shift ended, he skipped breakfast with the guys and headed to his place.

WITH DANIEL LEAVING for his car detailing job that morning, Sarah needed to show up early in order to have time to talk. Delaying the breakup for almost a week had eaten at her conscience, and she wanted it over with. First thing after waking up, she'd decided to tell him they could no longer be involved. No sense making things worse by admitting she loved him. Never mind it wasn't a full explanation. It was the best she could do without crumpling into a ball and making a fool of herself.

She fed Puff, then made her own breakfast. Not that she tasted a bite of it. After a quick shower, then wearing jeans and a sweater, she slipped into her coat and grabbed her purse. "I'll be back in a while," she told the kitten. She thought about letting Daniel know she was on her way over, but he probably figured as much.

At eight-thirty, trembling a little, she parked the Civic in front of his apartment building. Seconds later, she pressed the doorbell. In the time it took him to buzz her in, she almost decided to bag the whole thing and go home. Then there he was opening the door, also in jeans and a Carver's Detail T that clung to his shoulders. Her heart lifted at the sight of him, but she quickly got hold of herself.

"Come in," he said.

Not a smile in sight, in fact, he seemed as nervous as she was. As soon as she closed the door behind her, Toad hopped toward her, tail wagging. "Hi, you," she said, focusing on petting him instead of looking at Daniel.

She didn't take her coat off, as she wouldn't be there long. "Did you have a good time with your family?" she asked. "From what I saw, you seemed to."

"It was okay. Let's sit down and we'll talk."

"I think I'll stand," she said, shaking in her ankle boots. "I owe you an apology for my conduct Thursday. I didn't plan to act like that. I'd had two cocktails and I guess they interfered with my behavior." As awful and flimsy as that sounded, it was the best she could manage without getting into her feelings.

He wore the blank look that meant he'd hidden his emotions. "It was obvious you dumped me."

"I didn't mean to, not on Thanksgiving." He raised his eyebrows a fraction, waiting for her to go on, which wasn't making this easy. "There are times when my big mouth gets ahead of me," she floundered, hoping he'd put her out of her misery and say something.

"It's because we rushed into having sex, right? I never should've brought up the situationship thing."

Yes and no. He was right about the sex. If they hadn't made love, she wouldn't have fallen harder for him, and no, because she'd thoroughly enjoyed it. Not about to answer either way, she compressed her lips.

"Talk to me, Sarah. Please."

"I don't know what to say," she admitted.

"I thought we were happy together. I *know* we were. Is there nothing I can do to fix this?"

She saw the hurt in his eyes and felt terrible. "I don't think that's possible, Daniel."

"Tell me where I went wrong."

He wasn't at fault—she was. Knowing his heart belonged to Kendall and always would, she'd fallen for him anyway. She forced herself to look directly at him. "I can't answer that."

"Just say it, Sarah. I can take it. Do I have bad breath? Did I hurt your feelings or insult you somehow?"

"No," she answered in a timid voice she didn't recognize. She wanted to drop through a hole in the floor, but unfortunately, there were none.

Never-ending moments ticked by before he replied in a quiet but firm tone. "I won't accept your apology, not without your reason for doing this."

She felt sick. "I guess I deserve that."

"And I deserve for you to be straight with me."

Trembling at the unhappy male before her, she hugged herself, let out a heavy sigh, and caved. "All right, I'll tell you, but you won't like it." She forced herself to raise her head and focused on the smiling photo of him and Kendall. "The thing I said I wouldn't do has happened. I love you."

Afraid what she might see on his face, she turned away, quickly headed toward the door, and let herself out.

26

Even before the door closed behind Sarah, Daniel's jaw dropped. He knew she had feelings for him just as he did for her, but was gobsmacked. If she hadn't been in such a hurry to run away for the second time since Thanksgiving, she'd surely have seen the surprise on his face. Instead, she'd left without giving him a chance to say a single word. What kind of female confessed her love, then rushed out the door?

He'd never figured her as someone who ran away from a problem instead of facing it. Was she that afraid of him? He had no idea what he'd done to scare her like that.

His watch beeped, reminding him he had a car to detail. While he cleaned and buffed the red Mustang, he puzzled over the situation and what to do. He still didn't know the reason she'd pulled away from him, only that she had and that she loved him. A strange combo that made no sense. Damn her for that.

The shock of it left him feeling like he was standing on a thirty-foot high tightrope without a net. For the rest of the day he wandered around like a zombie, puzzling over his next moves. He took a long run with Toad, but nothing helpful came to mind, and he remained mystified and adrift.

The next day also went by in a daze. Friday, sick of his own company, he texted Rob and Tony and suggested they shoot hoops and then have lunch.

Rob texted that he was busy moving in with Jenny and the twins, and begged off. Tony gave him a call. "I'd take you up on the hoops thing and lunch, but I can't today. Summer and I are picking up stuff for the nursery and setting it up. I can talk for a little while, though. What's up?"

Grateful for his bud's time, Daniel told him about the truth bomb Sarah had dropped two days earlier.

"That's a new one," Tony said, and Daniel pictured him scratching his head.

"It's different, all right. The kicker is, she didn't give me a chance to respond—just told me and split so fast, you'd have thought she was running from a knife-carrying thug. Ever heard of a woman breaking up with a guy because she's in love with him?"

"Not even in the movies. Have you contacted her since?"

Daniel shook his head, but his buddy couldn't see that. "The way she lit out, like she couldn't get away fast enough? She doesn't want to hear from me." Thanksgiving had been painful enough. He wasn't up to dealing with yet another gut-wrenching rejection.

"I'm baffled," Tony said. "It's been a few days since it happened. How are you feeling now?"

Rudderless. In the short time Daniel had known her, she'd become his anchor, his confidant. But now, the connection that meant so much had been severed. "Like I lost a limb or worse." He scrubbed his hand over his face. "For the life of me, I can't figure out what to do now."

"That depends on what you want. Do you love her back?"

"I don't know, except that I want things to be like they were before."

"I'm no genius, but I know you can't go back, only forward. Gotta hang up now—Summer's ready to leave. Hang in there, buddy, and figure out what you want. Then go for it. See you Monday."

BEFORE WORK that same Friday morning, heartsick and miserable, Sarah texted Erin and asked her to come over for take-out after work. Between her overtime hours at the vet's and spending most nights at Flick's house, Erin hadn't been around much, and they hadn't communicated since Thanksgiving. Although Sarah had told Cherry and Mary Jo that she and Daniel weren't seeing each other anymore—afraid of sobbing, she'd refrained from sharing the details— Erin didn't even know that much.

Over take-out at the little house, with Puff napping on the couch, Sarah started the story. "I did it, broke things off with Daniel." Needless to say, she picked at the food.

"No wonder you're so messed up. When you love someone the way you do Daniel, getting over him is bound to take time. But please, take care of yourself. You need to eat or you'll waste away."

"Yes, mother," Sarah grumbled, but she picked up a fork for a taste. As it turned out, she was hungry and ate quite a bit. When she pushed the plate away, Erin nodded approvingly. "Satisfied now?"

"Someone had to remind you to put food in your mouth. Now I'm ready to hear about the breakup."

"I went to his house Wednesday morning and told him." Sarah stared at her tightly-clasped hands on the tabletop.

"You should've called me right away. I'd have come straight over when I clocked out."

"With all the overtime you've been working? I didn't want to bother you. Besides, I was too upset."

"If it were *me*, I'd bother *you*. Go on."

"When I left his house, I didn't expect to hear from him, and I haven't. It hurts anyway." Sarah blew out a heavy breath. "Pretty lame, huh? He's a good man, the total opposite of Jensen, but they're alike in one way. They're both allergic to the L word, at least from me. As soon as I used it, they disappeared from my life."

"You have a big heart, Sarah. It makes you kind and caring, and that's a beautiful thing." Erin angled her head as if puzzled about something. "I can't believe Daniel ghosted you. That doesn't sound at all like him"

Sarah hurried to correct the misinterpretation. "I didn't say he ghosted me—I said he hasn't been in touch."

"It's only been two days. He's probably lying low and licking his wounds like you are. What exactly did he do when you told him you loved him?"

"I didn't wait around to find out." She'd barely been able to hold herself together and was certain whatever he might have said, even a gentle rejection, would've ripped her to shreds.

Erin frowned. "Let's see if I have this right. You broke up with him, told him you love him, and then left without knowing what his reaction was?"

"I had to. He's still hung-up on his dead wife. I wasn't about to humiliate myself by breaking down in front of him. I have too much pride for that."

"In other words, you tried and convicted the man without giving him a chance to register what you said and respond."

Put that way, it sounded unfair. And maddeningly true. Sarah scowled. "Whose side are you on?"

"Hey, don't yell at me. I'm calling it as I see it, and what I see is your pride getting in the way of what could've been a meaningful conversation. You didn't give him a chance for that. I feel for him."

After mulling that over for a minute, Sarah agreed. "You're right, and I apologize for taking my misery out on you. I hadn't thought about it that way. But you didn't see the shock on his face when I used the L word." Recalling that brief glimpse, she hugged her waist. "It told me everything I needed to know. He's had a few days to think about things and hasn't contacted me. Does that sound like a man who truly cares? I don't think so." Erin didn't say anything, and Sarah added, "All I know is, I've never hurt like this. I really do love him."

"Then do something about it."

"He heard what I said. What else can I do?"

"Stop the pity party and take action. If you want the man in your life, reach out and talk to him."

News traveled fast, and during breakfast at the firehouse Monday morning, Daniel's team-mates weighed in with opinions about him and Sarah. Most of their advice echoed Tony's, which was no advice at all.

Dejected, he remained silent.

Ethan rubbed his chin. "She shared her feelings with you. I think you're in love with her, too."

So it seemed. Daniel shrugged.

"You're scared, huh?"

"Terrified."

"Here's a question for you," Rob chimed in. "How would you feel if she met someone else and forgot about you?"

He winced at the thought. "It'd kill me."

"Like it did me every time Jenny had more than one date with the same guy. Something to think about."

"Back up," Ethan said and scrutinized Daniel. "What are you afraid of?"

The room was super quiet, everyone looking at him. Not a question he wanted to answer, but he went ahead and did. "When my wife Kendall passed away, I wanted to die, too. It was a long time before I could function like a normal person. I feel rotten about the breakup with Sarah. But if I lost her like I did Kendall..." His voice cracked. Unable to finish, he shook his head.

Several heavy moments later, Tony weighed in. "One thing I've learned over the past year is that no matter who we are and what we do, there are times when life sucks. It can also be amazing. I can't say what might happen to you or to Sarah, but I know this for sure—if you don't do something, you'll lose her. Then your life will *really* suck."

Food for thought. Breakfast ended, and the team started the daily chores. Later that morning, there was a fire at a garage, followed by a grade-school kid having a seizure in the middle of class. Midafternoon, an elderly woman slipped and fell as she was walking outside. She blacked out and was taken to the hospital. All in all, a hectic day that kept Daniel's mind off his troubles. But they rolled around in his head.

That night in his bunk, despite the rest his body craved, he lay awake. He had a lot to think about. Certain things stood out—Izzy, saying that after Kendall passed on, she wished she'd asked Daniel questions instead of hiding her feelings, and promising that from now on, she'd let them out. Rob and Tony, both warning him that if he didn't do something, he'd lose Sarah for sure. If he didn't want that, he needed to act soon.

At the same time, Kendall was on his mind. At some point without realizing it, he'd stopped blaming himself for her death, and the heavy weight of guilt he'd carried had fallen away. Freed of that, he felt good. But other things bothered him. Days went by when he didn't think about her, and certain things about her had faded from his memory. He couldn't remember the sound of her voice or the little hiccup after she laughed really hard. Now, lying in his bunk, he talked to her. "I'm tired of feeling guilty about the past. I know the accident wasn't my fault and I'm going to let that go. I haven't known Sarah that long, but I have strong feelings for her. I want to be with her."

Once he shared his feelings, he fell into a deep, much-needed sleep. Mostly dreamless, until Kendall suddenly appeared with a message. "It's way past time you moved on," she advised. "You deserve to live a full life. Be happy and go after the woman you love."

She vanished and he jerked awake. Scrubbing the sleep from his eyes, he knew what he wanted and needed to do.

It was early, just after four a.m. Sarah would be heading to the dispatch center soon. Forget going back to sleep—which, now that he'd made up his mind, was impossible. Forget waiting till they were both off work tomorrow. This had to happen today. He pulled out his phone and texted her.

WHEN THE ALARM woke Sarah Tuesday morning, she felt different than when she'd gone to bed. At some point during the night she'd made a momentous decision: she wouldn't give up on Daniel without a fight. He was too important to her. She needed to see him and explain what she'd neglected to say when she'd hurried out of his house so abruptly almost a week ago. He deserved the full truth, warts and all, no matter what happened. If he rejected her, she'd know that at least she'd tried.

At this hour he was sleeping, but she had no

problem texting him, knowing he'd see the message when he woke up. She'd ask to see him as soon as her shift ended that afternoon.

As she worked on exactly what to say when they were face-to-face, her phone signaled an incoming text from him. Talk about a coincidence. Instead of reading it, she phoned. "Believe it or not, I was just texting you," she said. "You're up early. Bad night?"

He didn't answer the question or start with any pleasantries. "We need to talk ASAP. Can you stop by the firehouse after work?"

"Funny, my message to you was about the same thing," she said, wondering what he wanted to say and why he couldn't say it over the phone. "I'll be there." She crossed her fingers he wouldn't be called away on an emergency.

He disconnected. Did he have to hang up without even a hint of what this was about? Of course, she shared the news with Mary Jo and Cherry. Like her, they were breathless with curiosity. If he wanted to see her, it couldn't be bad.

Could it?

Needless to say, she spent the day on pins and needles, until at long last she clocked out and headed for the station. A bundle of nerves, she arrived and parked. Sitting in her car, she texted Daniel that she was there and heading for the lobby. Then she went inside.

Miranda's shift ended an hour after hers, and she expected to greet the woman at the front desk, then wait for him to show up. To her surprise, he was already there. After what seemed forever since she'd last set eyes on him, she drank in the sight. The big, fit, handsome man she was about to humble herself to, sharing the part of herself she least liked and explaining the real reason she'd broken things off.

"Hey," he said. No smiles, just a nod. "We'll be in the conference room, Miranda. Don't bother us unless it's an emergency."

All eyes, the woman nodded, a smile hovering on her lips.

Clinging to the thought that the secretary/receptionist wouldn't look so pleased if it was bad news, never mind that she had no idea what was going on, Sarah followed him into the big room where the team had group meetings and trainings.

Once inside the room, he shut the door.

"I—" she started.

"What I—" he said at the same time.

"Let me go first, please," she said, straightening her shoulders to bolster her courage. He might not understand, but he deserved to know what a needy person she'd been, and how ashamed of herself she was.

"All right." He gestured at a chair, then sat in the adjacent seat.

Wishing she had a glass of water, she cleared her throat. "I haven't been entirely honest with you," she started. His face gave away nothing, and she continued. "When I told you about Jensen, I left something out that I'm still embarrassed to admit. I was so needy and desperate to hold on to him that I told him I loved him. I thought it might help. I was wrong. He couldn't get away from me fast enough." Now for the worst part. "Deep down, I'd expected that, but I wasn't ready for him to walk away. I pleaded with him to stay and talk." She bit her lip, remembering. "A lame, last-ditch effort that failed. He looked at me with disgust and walked out."

She was still so mortified that her cheeks went hot

with shame. "What I regret most about that night is the utter fool I made of myself when I begged him not to go. Then and there, I swore I'd never be that vulnerable again or use the L word first."

There, it was out. Pulling in a breath, she braced for his reaction, whatever it might be. By his scrunched-up forehead, he was confused.

"But you said the L word to me. Then you ran away."

"I don't consider what I did 'running away.' I'll explain in a minute. You asked for an explanation, and it was only fair to give you one. You've been honest from the beginning about Kendall. She's the woman you love. Yet, there I was, loving you when I knew my feelings wouldn't be reciprocated. Still, I owed you the truth, so I deprecated myself and told you I loved you. Once I admitted it, I couldn't bear to face you. I saw your shocked expression and left before I humiliated myself even more." She started to duck his gaze, but instead forced herself to look straight at him. "That's why I left so quickly. Now that you know, I'll leave you to your evening." She stood.

"Uh-uh—you don't get to cut and run this time," he said, taking her hands and gently pulling her back onto the chair. "I have a few things of my own to say, remember?"

Reliving the nauseating story of her past had chilled her, and her hands were ice-cold, but he didn't comment. Which was either a positive sign or his way of letting her down easy because he felt sorry for her. She braced for the worst. "Go ahead."

"I was surprised, not shocked, when you said you'd fallen for me. I was also baffled. Why would you break up with me if you loved me? That didn't make sense, and I needed a minute to figure you out. But you never gave me a chance. If you'd waited a little longer, you'd have heard me say that I have strong feelings for you, too. I wasn't ready to put a name to them. First, I needed to tell Kendall."

He searched her face and it was her turn to wonder what he was getting at. "Oh?"

"Sometimes I talk to her, which probably sounds crazy. It's something I do when I'm working out a problem and struggling to put the situation into words. I know I'm really talking to myself, but it helps me. I'll always love her, but in a different way than when she was alive. I've been telling her about you. I know she wants what's best for me. That means you, Sarah. I love you back."

She promptly burst into tears.

He gaped at her. "Uh-oh."

"I just—you love me?"

"I do."

She threw her arms around him. "This is a dream come true."

"I like that, and I love you." He tipped up her chin and kissed her. And she was home. Several sizzling kisses later, he pulled away and smoothed her hair. "At times both of us can be real screwballs, huh? Let's make a pact to be more open with each other from now on. If something doesn't sit well with either of us, we talk about it together. Deal?"

Her heart brimmed with love and joy. "Only if we seal our pact with a kiss."

He grinned. "If you insist..."

She stretched up to meet him. "I do have one more confession," she said, when she reluctantly pulled away a short time later. "I've loved you from the day I first saw you." She paused. "That's not quite true. At first, it was a crush."

He shook his head. "I had no idea."

"We rarely saw each other, and I figured I'd get over it. Then at Rosemary's the morning we discussed your upcoming training and you smiled, my crush grew. Before long, it turned into love. Now you know everything."

His eyes beamed warmth and feeling. "I wish we could be alone for a few hours."

"Me too, but I don't think sex in the conference room is appropriate."

"Guess we'll have to wait, then. Hey, why don't we have breakfast at Rosemary's tomorrow? I want the guys to see us together."

"They've seen us before."

"Not like this. I want them to know you're my woman."

"And you're my guy."

He kissed her again. "On second thought, scrap the breakfast-out idea. Why don't I come to your place in the morning? I have to pick up Toad from Jenny's first and he'll be with me, if that's good with you. The time I brought him along when I looked in on Puff, they got along okay. I suspect in the future, they'll be seeing a lot more of each other."

"I'm sure of it. I'll make us breakfast."

The fire alarm rang, ending the conversation. "See you in the morning," Daniel said, and hightailed out of the room.

"Be safe," she called after him. She pictured him rushing downstairs toward the fire engine, his crewmates, and the turnout clothes and shoes he needed. Lingering in the conference room and excited to share what'd happened, she phoned Erin. Her friend didn't pick up—still at work—and she left a voice mail. "Guess what? Daniel loves me! Fill you in later."

She left similar messages on Mary Jo and Cherry's phones.

Next, she shared the good news with Elton. He was out with his girlfriend, but pleased to hear the update. Finally, she e-mailed her parents, who were somewhere in the Caribbean.

She still had things to discuss with Daniel—their views of the future, if there was one, whether either of them wanted marriage. Then there was the kids question—she wanted them, but had no idea about him. Lots of other unknowns, too, but they had plenty of time to find out.

The only thing she knew with certainty was that Daniel loved her the way she'd always dreamed of. She spent the rest of the evening playing with Puff and floating on air.

28

Whistling and happier than he'd been in a long time, Daniel arrived at Sarah's Wednesday morning with Toad and treats from Rosemary's.

"A man after my own heart," she murmured, after showering him with kisses.

He didn't think he'd ever get tired of that. "If treats are what it takes to get more of those, I'm in," he teased, while Puff and Toad traded wary looks. "Be nice—you two have met," he reminded them.

"That's right," Sarah seconded. "At least she's not hissing at him. Did the fire last night keep you up?"

"Lucky for us all, it didn't. A couple of teens got together and one of them decided to try out the fire pit his parents had recently installed. The adults were at a party and hadn't yet taught him the right way to use it. The fire got out of hand, and the kids panicked and called 911."

"At least they knew who to call. What happened then?"

"By the time we arrived, it was mostly out. Good thing it's winter—there isn't much foliage right now.

The only damage was a charred patch of ground nearby."

"Those kids really lucked out."

"Not exactly. We contacted the parents. They came straight home, and their son is grounded till January."

"Live and learn." She glanced at the animals and lowered her voice. "Check those two out." Except for the wagging tail, Toad held still while Puff sashayed toward him. He gave his friendly *woof*, she meowed, and they did what pets do—sniffed and got to know each other better.

Taking advantage of the moment, Daniel pulled Sarah in to a hug. "Speaking of getting to know each other better, why don't we do the same?" He tipped up her chin, and they shared passionate kisses that soon escalated. "I don't think Puff and Toad are in danger of harming each other. Let's make love now and eat breakfast after."

"Excellent idea."

Sometime later, lying together sated and more relaxed than he'd been in years, he rested his palm on her hip and snuggled her closer. "I love you, Sarah McCone."

"Love you back. By the way, I told Erin, Mary Jo, and Cherry at the dispatch center. Also Elton and my parents. I told my mom I want to have a closer relationship, and we're going to work on that when they get back. I hope you don't mind that I shared the news about us."

"Not at all. Everyone at the station knew about us last night. I called my parents and said I might bring you home for Christmas, if you want to spend the holiday with my family, and yours are okay with that."

"Lee and Mason are so pleased for us, I'm sure they will be. We'll go to my folks' place next year."

Daniel's stomach rumbled and she kissed his belly. "Sounds like breakfast time."

Over coffee and muffins, they discussed things they hadn't before. "Have Erin and her boyfriend found a place to live?" he asked.

"Not as far as I know. Why?"

"Asking in case you can't find a decent roommate."

She grinned. "Are you volunteering?"

"Maybe. "

"Ah, you'd rather be a roommate than a married man."

"I didn't say that."

"I distinctly remember a conversation where you said you weren't interested in another marriage."

He rubbed his chin. "Did I? Huh. Since you brought up the subject, what do you think about marriage, Sarah?"

"You answer that first."

"I'm interested."

She kissed him lightly. "Good, because I definitely want it, but it's too soon."

Not for him. He finally understood why so many of his firefighter brothers moved in with their girlfriends. Sarah owned his heart. "I want you now and forever, but if you'd rather wait, fine with me." With her hair down and tangled and her skin flushed after their unbelievably fine sex, she was the most beautiful woman ever. He wanted her again. "I've been fantasizing about a shower together. You in?"

A wicked smile lit her face. "I could be enticed—if you make it worthwhile."

"You know I will."

She glanced toward the living room, where the two animals napped close to each other, and beamed. "They're so cute together!"

Lazing about after the shower, they discussed the future. "I want kids," he said, playing with her silky hair. "How about you?"

"Absolutely, but not right away. For now, I want you all to myself."

He tucked the hair behind the ears of the woman he loved. "You have yourself a deal."

ALSO BY ANN ROTH

Port Simms

Book 1: Who's Getting Married?

Book 2: Maybe This Time

Ann Roth Classics

A Place to Belong

Father of the Year

Another Life

My Sisters

Dunlin Shores

Book 1: Just the Way You Are

Book 2: Wedding Bell Blues

Book 3: Falling for Mr. Wrong

Book 4: A Special Kind of Love

Firefighters

Book 1: Mr. January

Book 2: Mr. February

Book 3: Mr. March

Book 4: Mr. April

Book 5: Mr. May

Book 6: Mr. June

Book 7: Mr. July

Book 8: Mr. August

Book 9: Mr. September

Book 10: Mr. October

Book 11: Mr November

Book 12: Mr. December

Halo Island

Book 1: All I Want for Christmas

Book 2: The Pilot's Woman

Book 3: Ooh, Baby!

Book 4: The One I Love

Miracle Falls

Book 1: Christmas in Miracle Falls

Book 2: Dream a Little Dream

Book 3: It Had to Be You

Book 4: You're the One That I Want

Book 5: There's Something About You

Book 6: My Heart Belongs to You

Saddlers Prairie

Book 1: Since I Fell for You

Book 2: I'll Be There

Book 3: Until There Was You

Book 4: Got My Heart Set On You

ABOUT THE AUTHOR

Ann Roth is an award-winning author of 40-plus contemporary romance and women's fiction novels, as well as novellas and numerous short stories. Her first novel was published in 2000 by Harlequin Special Edition and was nominated by *Romantic Times* as best first book. Ann lives with the love of her life in the Greater Seattle area and enjoys creating flawed characters and putting them in challenging situations that help them grow and ultimately find love— whether or not they're looking for it.

Find out about new releases!
Sign up for my newsletter

Or visit my website www.annroth.net